The Luck of the Fall

The Luck
of the Fall

Jim Ray Daniels

MICHIGAN STATE UNIVERSITY PRESS | *East Lansing*

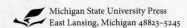 Michigan State University Press
East Lansing, Michigan 48823–5245

LIBRARY OF CONGRESS CATALOGING-IN-PUBLICATION DATA
Names: Daniels, Jim, 1956– author.
Title: The luck of the fall / Jim Ray Daniels.
Description: East Lansing : Michigan State University Press, 2023.
Identifiers: LCCN 2023001808 | ISBN 978-1-61186-467-0 (paperback) |
ISBN 978-1-60917-744-7 | ISBN 978-1-62895-509-5
Subjects: LCGFT: Short stories.
Classification: LCC PS3554.A5635 L83 2023 |
DDC 813/.54—dc23/eng/20230120
LC record available at https://lccn.loc.gov/2023001808

Cover design by Erin Kirk
Cover art: Adobe Stock | Creaturart

Visit Michigan State University Press at *www.msupress.org*

Contents

The Luck of the Fall

October's streetlight had not yet thrown its damp-blanket chill over us on Pearl Street, but it had given notice—the cold in the back of our throats that signaled change. On our drab street of tract three-bedroom ranches surrounding the Ford plant on Eight Mile Road on the edge of Detroit, a single tree had been planted uniformly in the middle of each tiny, ragged lawn. The series of dotted i's down the street—maple, oak, maple, oak—had yet to fill out, and, in fact, many had already died and not been replaced, as if the dots had been an unnecessary frill of punctuation. As dusk fell, the small clusters of changing leaves resembled small campfires until darkness snuffed them out entirely.

When our fathers weren't working overtime, we all ate at 5:30. If someone had a dinner bell, they could safely ring it at that hour and bring all the children in the neighborhood home to wash our hands and say grace and wolf down whatever pale meat or overcooked spaghetti or other dried-then-boxed or frozen-then-thawed or canned substance fried or boiled or heated up in a saucepan. We were proud of our uniform blandness—we leaned against it

1

for comfort. The only fish we ate had been bullied into squares, breaded and frozen, so we never connected what swam to what we consumed. Even during Lent, when we abstained from meat and tackled fish and chips on Fridays from the K of C in their squeaky Styrofoam containers, the fish was disguised by the Rorschach-test shapes of thick breading.

My friend Cathy's dog Fishstick bit me on the ring finger of my left hand, leaving a scar below the knuckle as a warning to never get married or maybe just never reach too quickly for anything. To wait my turn and take what was given without expectation.

•••

If you looked out our front window, you could see Paula and Cathy, both eleven, a year younger than me, sprawled in the slightly damp grass, cool to the touch, practicing cheers on Paula's front lawn in the after-dinner in-between—they lived three doors down from each other. Careless laughter and imprecise cartwheels. They'd never be cheerleaders—we probably all knew that. They'd both get pregnant in high school—none of us imagined that. I was a young idiot-boy who had known them from birth and couldn't handle the shade their pregnancies threw on our street. It stung me hard and deep, like a long breath of that new chill air.

•••

The Ford plant turned our fathers into worker ants on the ant hill and our mothers into worker ants in the neighborhood. We lived in a company town without a town—the frontier of the Ford plant—the Great Prairie, and we were all prairie dogs—the . . . Oh, forget it. I'm lost on my way across the street to cheer the cheerleaders. They knew all the routines by heart, despite their lack of pompoms, uniforms, and the untouchable wholesome aura of the official cheerleaders who cheered on the official football players under the lurid glare of the lights on the Eight Mile High football field that we could see from our sidewalk, hulking over the low shoulders of our tiny houses.

Our neighborhood guys played tackle football without pads in the swampy field on the edge of the woods next to Schofield Elementary on weekend afternoons. In the street, we played two-hand touch. Two-hand shove. Everything and nothing out of bounds. We beat on each other out of reckless affection or subconscious preparation for our assembly-line futures. Our favorite game was Free-For-All, a brutal game without rules in which we jumped on each other, falling into a ragged pile, randomly fighting until someone got hurt. Fun, we called it, unleashing our pent-up whatever on the anonymous streets of identical houses. We'd never play for the school team. That required anonymous haircuts and sincerity. That required faith in their scoreboard.

•••

Our families each had one car, and those cars were driven daily on the giant sea of asphalt called Eight Mile Road, gashed by yellow lines so everyone knew their places, where to dock their dinghies.

Despite our inability to circle our station wagons, we turned inward with unspoken love and outward with spoken defiance. On our block, we did not judge. *Tough luck*, we said softly to those girls as their bellies rounded, our heads tilting toward them, since we never spoke the words *I love you* to anyone. We wanted to gently touch those bellies, but we were shy and afraid and maybe superstitious about that luck.

None of the school's cheerleaders got pregnant. I think their advisor, Mrs. Fountain, provided them with more useful advice and perhaps even some concrete forms of protection. Or perhaps they were not even—no, they had to be.

•••

We never found a four-leafer in our weedy lawns, though they included plenty of clover. We all knew the stupid trick of squeezing two stems together so it looked like four leaves, yet we could not stop ourselves from doing it. Or from rubbing dandelions under our necks to see if we liked butter or were in love or both. I learned later that it was supposed to be buttercups, a kind of flower. All I know is that if you rub dandelions hard enough, they can turn anything yellow.

•••

We kissed that evening, the three of us, careless as those cartwheels, on that ragged grass beginning its brown journey, uncut since Labor Day. They took turns kissing me and laughing, sprawling away onto their backs, then leaning in again. Our cold noses and fingers touched. Jazzed up by proximity and darkness, we bristled in our thin fall jackets. By newfound strength and range of motion. By curious tingling, the static electricity of the startling awareness of opposites. Cold noses, warm cheeks.

•••

"Hey, what are you guys doing?" I asked.

"Cheers, what do you think?"

"Yeah," I nodded. I was no wise guy with words. How we got to kissing, I'm still not sure. I plopped down on the grass, and they plopped down too. As if we were slipping beneath some invisible wire, escaping unsnagged. I could hear Fishstick barking at the fence three doors down.

"Fishstick's lonely," Cathy said.

"He shouldn't be biting people then," Paula said, and she grabbed my hand where it pushed into the grass. I lost my balance and fell flat on my back. "Let's see that finger," Paula said. The scab was hardening and narrowing into what would be its permanent scar. "I'll kiss your boo-boo," she said.

"No, I'll kiss your boo-boo. It was my dog," Cathy said, and they laughed and fell, wrestling on top of me, twisting my arm around so we got all tangled and touching, and then we stopped and breathed heavily enough to warm each other's faces. That might have been enough for any other cool October evening in our back catalog. But it wasn't enough on this night. Sweet clover breath caressed my face as we lay stunned and chilled, magnifying the double digits of our young hearts.

Who kissed who first didn't matter much once we started. Soon, they were swiveling my head back and forth to alternate kissing my chapped lips, each of them trying to outdo the other in duration and exaggerated smacking that soon faded into something quieter, more serious. Me, I did no smacking at all.

•••

Paula was pale, blonde, and thin. Her long hair flew as we rolled laughing and kissing across the lawn. Hair falling into the open mouth of laughter. Fierce eyes exposed as she brushed it away to kiss me again.

Paula's nose was always red and running. Her eyes developed serious dark circles under them, like judgmental ashes, after she got pregnant. The rest of her seemed to shrink as her belly swelled. A few months in, she disappeared entirely. She finally showed up again, alone, childless. She never finished high school. The last time I saw her was in a "drug store," the kind we both came to haunt in later days.

•••

I'd like to stop with us staring at each other in the light of the bare-bulb lamp on the naked floor of that abandoned house that had been repurposed for drugs, but it'd make the end predictable, easy. I can't describe my eyes then, but hers—recognition, but no affect. It was like *Oh, you too.* Our old neighborhood had turned into the shooting game at the bowling alley where we hung out during our early teens. One of those old western shoot-'em-ups. Ping. Ping. The goal: shoot all the bad guys in the allotted time. If you accomplished that, you got extra time to shoot more bad guys.

The faceless bad guys closed the Ford plant. We could not shoot them, so we shot each other until houses were abandoned by our parents, or by us, depending on who was still alive and had their wits about them.

•••

Cathy's older brother Kevin was my friend, so I hung out at their house. Fishstick loved Kevin but never liked me, despite us looking alike—some kids at school even called us brothers.

Cathy's long brown hair, turned up at the ends, bounced when she walked. An enthusiastic walker, she sprung up from the sidewalk with each step. Her cartwheels were spectacular in their messy sprawl. When she started shuffling down the street with the weight of her "sin," it was all the sadder. Cathy came back and finished school, then left town. Kevin says she's doing cartwheels again somewhere in the UP. I hope she doesn't get buried in snow up there.

We learned as we got into more advanced math that many of our parents had married due to unplanned pregnancies. Holy Helen—the outlier as the mother of only one child—lived at the end of the block, but no one paid her wagging finger much attention. She was like a commandment we forgot to memorize. We all went to the same church and listened to the same sermons—just Sunday background noise for our lives, one more thing we had to put up with. When it came to getting married or buried, we called up the church, and they took care of things in exchange for cash money.

•••

We on Pearl Street rarely got to decide when to stop anything. Money and power give you more control over stopping. Free-For-Alls only stopped when someone got hurt.

That might have been a good place to at least pause a while longer: two pretty girls kissing me without consequence on a clear night in October as the sky went from dark blue to black. A few rare stars may have even been visible, though, if so, we weren't paying them any mind. The gray fuzz of our polluted skies mirroring our concrete streets provided some comfort and insulation against the deeper plunge of lost possibilities. Maybe we should have looked up a little more often.

•••

"I don't want to be a cheerleader," Paula said.

"Nobody said you did," Cathy said.

"How come they don't have guy cheerleaders?" I asked, just to contribute, as we worked to fill the silence of not knowing what to do next.

"Some schools do," Cathy said, "like, colleges."

"Show us what you got," Paula said, and they both snorted.

I laughed too. I had nothing to show.

"I feel the earth spinning," I said. "Through the ground. Real slow."

"That's because we're such good kissers," Cathy said. I lay there, my skin suddenly prickly, wanting to say something clever, but my mouth was dry, and I felt something weird in my chest, so I just swallowed, then murmured, "Maybe you're right" as if I knew a thing about kissing.

Cathy reached over the cool, damp grass we'd matted down with our wrestling. She grabbed my hand and squeezed, so I reached over and grabbed Paula's hand and squeezed. On her front lawn, behind the thin pine tree that had done so well that someone would cut it down and steal it for Christmas that year. A lesson in that for all of us that we'd learn over and over: anything nice will disappear.

The Spirit Award

To say Jack was disappointed was to say *it looks like it might rain* while it was already streaming off the brim of your new baseball hat. He walked to his father's car, trailing him by a good six feet. His father always walked fast, but tonight he seemed to have completely forgotten he wasn't alone, that he believed he'd done his duty and was dismissed from further obligation, when in fact he'd completely blown off his duty, which was to go to Jack's eighth-grade sports banquet, to be The Dad for a few minutes, to stand and joke with other proud fathers. He'd arrived for the closing remarks, just in time to take Jack home for the weekend.

From behind, Jack watched his father's limber long-legged walk, the tight shoulders and thick neck of a former athlete. For someone always in a hurry, his father had sure been showing up late a lot, or not showing up at all. "Dad, wait up," he wanted to say. Or, simply "Dad." To get him to stop. To wait. Forced into frantic half-running, trying to keep up, Jack did a full frontal onto the sidewalk, scraping both hands. When he was younger, he could've started wailing, and his father would have come back to lift him into his arms.

His mother had dropped him off—Jack didn't even know where his father had parked. He had missed the Spirit Award, so he couldn't share his son's disappointment. What was the hurry? What would they do back at his new apartment but watch TV? His father had a new girlfriend—Missy or Misty. He had moved out just three months ago, breaking up his *second* family—he'd had two kids with his first wife. The new girlfriend—a younger clone of his mother—creeped Jack out. Same long black hair, same angular face. His mother's was still twisted into the tight pain of rage. Jack had felt guilty relief when she'd dropped him off.

His stepsisters from his father's first marriage now spent all their time with their own mother, though they'd had a bedroom to share at Jack's house. Now that their father had moved out, why would the girls stay there, related to no one, no longer step-anything? Everything he'd been leaning on seemed to be toppling over. It was all too fucking confusing for an eighth grader. Maybe he didn't get the Spirit Award for thinking things like that: *fuck, fuck, fucking fuck*. He balled up the flimsy certificate in his hand. The one they all received simply for being on the team. His name was on it, so he couldn't toss it in the street so close to school. Someone might retrieve it and try to give it back.

•••

The Spirit Award was given to the player who was kindest, most unselfish, who contributed the most to team spirit. The consolation prize for benchwarmers—a throwaway award—but Jack had been counting on it. The thought of it got him through the last half of the season when the coach started using more sixth and seventh graders off the bench to get ready for next year.

Last year, Albert Cooper got the Spirit Award. He had sat next to Jack on the bench, providing a running commentary on the life of Albert Cooper, future superstar. Albert rarely noticed what was happening on the court. Overweight and slow, he had deluded himself into thinking he was one of the guys, that the only reason he never managed to get in the games was because the coach was saving him for the right moment. Albert had gone on to St. Joe's, the top sports high school in suburban Detroit, where he hadn't even made the team. How did he get that award? Jack wondered. Were his parents big donors?

The Wallingford School had a no-cut policy, but that didn't mean everyone played. Jack's problem: he was short, but played tall. He had little ball-handling skill. Intense and aggressive, he'd been good at getting rebounds until everyone else had their growth spurts. Coach Reynolds called him a throwback. Coach Reynolds always praised his hustle. Coach Reynolds had betrayed him, just like his father.

•••

"Now, I'd like to present this year's Spirit Award. We had a great group of kids this year, and it was a hard call. This young man never missed a practice. He worked hard, day in and day out. He was always there cheering his teammates on. Terry, c'mon up here. Terry Christopher."

Jack slumped in the stiff wooden folding chair so that it cut into his back. He put a hand to his forehead and rubbed it fiercely. The other boys all sat with at least one parent. Some even had a grandparent or two. Jack sat at a table with Artie Trappelli's family. He heard soft groans from some other players, a slight hesitation before polite applause. Terry never missed a practice because his dad was assistant coach. Throughout the season, he had gotten more playing time than he deserved. Spirit, my ass, thought Jack. Coach Christopher had to know his son didn't deserve the award. Terry once told Jack that he wanted to quit the team but his father wouldn't let him.

While the rest of the awards were being given out, Jack wolfed down three hotdogs and two bags of chips, staring at the ketchup-smeared paper plate in front of him, that bloody clock face without hands. He wanted to make himself sick. He'd stopped looking for his father.

Artie Trappelli smacked him in the back of the head as he walked past at the end of the banquet—Artie, MVP, high scorer, who'd been bouncing up to get awards all evening. What did that smack mean? It could've meant, "I know you got screwed, buddy." He sure wasn't going to say, "Jack, you are a thoughtful guy, and I appreciate your kindness and spirit." Jack failed to stifle a burp, wiped his face with his balled-up napkin, and hurried to the bathroom.

He was standing at the urinal when Coach Reynolds came out of the stall to wash his hands. Jack stared straight ahead, at risk of choking into tears. The coach was taking his time, using multiple paper towels. He sighed. Jack zipped up and headed toward the second sink.

"Well, Jack?" the coach said, turning as he grabbed the door handle. "Did you get enough to eat?"

Jack couldn't speak. He shook his head *no*. The coach was already halfway out the door.

•••

"This young man—this young man"—Jack lay in bed imagining the speech the coach should've given. If his father had come to some games, maybe Coach Reynolds would've felt pressure to be fair. If he saw that someone cared about Jack. Someone who knew a thing about sports, who had the good looks and charm and confidence of an old jock who kept in shape, who got the girls, who had a good job, who had influence, tickets to the big game, who knew somebody who knew somebody. His dad had played college ball. You could just look at him and tell. When he put his hand on your shoulder, you felt blessed by good fortune. Jack had seen it all his life. But Jack's dad was busy squandering that charm, tossing family number two to the curb. And women—women felt something too. But Coach Reynolds wouldn't have let himself get schmoozed by a slick guy like his dad. Would he?

Since everybody expected Jack to be angry when his father left him and his mother, he hadn't known how to show his displeasure in a way that might surprise someone into paying attention. No way could he match his mother's rage. He was at a difficult age, everybody said. His teachers had been alerted.

His grandparents had pitched in with supportive phone calls and generic greeting cards loaded with cash. He was pretty sure Hallmark didn't have a line of cards for his situation.

How about a card saying, *Sorry you didn't get the Spirit Award. You are OUR Spirit Award winner*! Exclamation point. He needed a lot of exclamation points. Jack had hoped at least one teammate would acknowledge he'd been jobbed by the old boy network. Everybody was going on to different high schools. The end of the line for them as a team, and no one was going to invest any outrage in a consolation prize for benchwarmers. That was as true as any statistic.

...

Coach Reynolds had put his arm around him after Jack had scored his lone basket of the season. He was always pointing out Jack as the model: "Look at Stern here, he's not complaining. Look at Stern here, he's ready to go in and take your place. Look at Stern running sprints—he's not dogging it."

One late afternoon, Jack sat alone in the bleachers after practice, waiting for a ride—in the confusion of his parents' separation, his pickup had slipped off the charts.

Coach said, "I wish they could all be like you, Jackie," as he headed out of the gym. Jack got choked up: nobody appreciated him, but coach did.

"Look at Stern, he got enough to eat." Jack wanted to say something to coach about the award, but what could he say that wouldn't make him a sore loser? Wouldn't make all his spirit seem like an act now, like one of his father's acts?

...

He could hear his father and Misty giggling in their bedroom. Misty was an airhead—even Jack knew that. She had no idea how to deal with children. She spoke to him in this sing-songy voice that perhaps she used for her cats. How could his father dump his mother for this? Dump *him*, for *this*? Jack wanted to compare notes with his ex-stepsisters, but they hadn't returned his texts.

Jack took eight shots all season, and made one. He took two free throws, and missed both. He committed twelve personal fouls. He pulled down fourteen rebounds. Zero steals. Two turnovers. He needed more statistics to put himself to sleep, more numbers. More proof. The Spirit Award—no stats for good behavior.

He had never heard his mother giggle like Misty was giggling. Maybe he would've needed to be around before he was born to hear that.

•••

Dad, wait up. You can't leave Mom like you left your first wife. Don't make me stay in your little apartment listening to you and Misty. Is that her real name? Who ever heard of someone named Misty?

Finally, his father turned around to look for him. Jack held up his hand. "Dad, wait up." He could say it now that his father had turned.

"C'mon, Jack, it's late." His father looked at his watch in a showy display. Other kids and their parents were passing by, getting in cars, slamming doors. The cold March rain still had some winter in it. Jack had turned his phone off for the ceremony and missed his father's call saying he was running late.

When Jack caught up to him, his father quickly turned and hurried in front again like a game they used to play when Jack was a boy. He was no longer a boy. Nobody seemed to see that. His father had been fucking Missy for how long? Jack wasn't an idiot. Jack could see his father's slick black sports car shining wet under a streetlight. His father, pushing fifty, driving a car that could not even hold all his children.

"Your father's whole life's been one long midlife crisis," his mother had said. What did it mean to be at midlife? Maybe *he* was at midlife? Would he die at twenty-eight? Jack scrambled into the passenger seat after his father popped the lock. He buckled up.

...

"You going to play high school ball?" his father asked. The hot dogs and Cokes and chips sloshing in Jack's stomach as his father shifted gears over the wet streets blurred with passing headlights, streetlights, stoplights, emergency flashers. Silence in the car, but outside, a chaos of lights.

"I was hoping to get an award tonight."

"You got a certificate or something, didn't you?"

Jack crumpled it tighter in his fist.

"Everybody gets certificates, Dad."

"Yeah, right," his father said.

"But I stuck it out," Jack said. "That means something." He waited for confirmation.

"Yeah, you stuck it out," his father finally said, nearly snorting.

When Jack was younger, his father had coached his Boy's Club team, but like many fine athletes, he didn't have the patience to teach others who did not have his gifts. He showed off at practice, draining three pointers from all around the arc. When it came to instruction, he told them what *not* to do, but not what to do if they couldn't do what he'd been able to.

Still, Jack had liked that time together, away from his mother and stepsisters. Getting in the car together like they were a team, like they could do something, the two of them. Make a dent together in the impenetrable ordinary world.

His father sighed louder than the heater dishing it out full blast. "Listen, I'm sorry I couldn't make it. Okay?"

"To what, my life?" Jack shouted abruptly. The rain was pouring down. The wipers couldn't keep up. If the temperature dropped any lower, it'd be snowing.

His father downshifted to slow the car. "Settle down, now. Just because you didn't get some award."

"You never come to anything. All the other fathers—"

"When's the last time your mother came to one of your games?"

"Mom hates sports."

"She didn't used to."

Jack tried to think of a comeback. Maybe she'd been taken in by his jock appeal, though she was a lawyer like him, someone not easily taken in by surface luster. "My life"—that'd been a good one. His mother was no longer a good sport.

Jack's father specialized in liquor licenses. He knew every restaurant owner in town. He ate well. He drank well. He got bored easily.

"Your mother and I . . ." his father began.

"What did you say to Cheryl and Kim?"

"Your mother and I . . ."

"I mean, last time you did this. I bet they got a kick out of hearing you did it again."

"This is *this* time. That's all that should matter to you. Your father has commitment issues, okay? I'm never getting married again, okay?"

"You tell Missy that?"

"Misty—"

His father clutched and shifted again.

"You going to be making any babies with her?"

His father made a noise like a barked laugh. "Sometimes, life just gets away from you."

"Dad, you've got everything. Am I supposed to feel sorry for you?"

Jack didn't want to deal with his father like this. His father playing the human-being card on him, making him talk like a grown up when he wasn't even in high school.

"No, I just don't want you expecting me to feel sorry for *you* because you didn't get—what award? I didn't think you played much."

Jack hesitated. He looked over at water streaming down the side window. "The Spirit Award."

"Aw, Jack," his father said, "that's . . . that's a chump award, isn't it? You don't need that crap. You've got the rest of your life—sitting on the bench and being a good sport isn't going to cut it."

"I wanted—I deserved that award. The assistant coach's kid got it."

"Okay. Okay, so you learned—everything's a rigged deal. That's a good thing to figure out now, not later when somebody screws you out of a job or a contract."

"What was rigged about being married to Mom—who got screwed on that one?"

"You don't have to play next year."

"I didn't have to play this year." Jack thought it would feel better, mouthing off to his father, but he just felt sick. Hot dogs and Coke and chips and his father. He tried to jam the certificate into the pocket of his suit coat, but it was sewn shut. He sat on it instead. He *did* want his father to feel sorry for him, and what was wrong with that?

"Why the hell do they sew the pockets shut on these things?"

"See, that's the kind of question you need to be asking," his father said, pointing vaguely out toward the rain.

...

Jack's father rented a new apartment in downtown Detroit, a completely kid-unfriendly place above a rehabbed theater. Being a good sport would never get his parents back together. Losing gracefully just made it easier for the winners, and what was the point of that?

Jack wondered if the other guys shunned him because the coach used him as the good example. Maybe the coach himself had disdain for a kid who wanted to please that badly.

They parked in the garage next to his father's building. The rain slanted in sideways through the gaps between pillars, and the wind howled through the cold cement tunnel between buildings. Jack shuddered, his sport coat and tie flapping as he ran to the elevator, ahead of his father now, who was running to catch up, to say one more thing.

"Your mother's no innocent in all this," he nearly shouted. "She knew what the deal was going in. Don't let her turn you against me."

"Did I know what the deal was?" He did not have to be a good teammate ever again. He let the elevator door close just as his father was about to enter.

Misty buzzed him in. She sat bundled up in a blanket like a fluffy kitten, her dark hair stark against the new white overstuffed couch.

"How was the banquet, Jackie?" she asked with all the enthusiasm of an auditioning cheerleader.

"Okay," Jack said, and tossed his wet sports coat to the floor. Just then his father stormed in, glaring.

"Come and sit down, tell me all about it," Misty said, patting the cushion next to her. "All grown up in your fancy clothes."

"It's okay, Misty, you don't have to . . ." his father said. She looked like she was about to say something, but his father repeated firmly, "It's okay. Jack can handle it. He's a big boy with a lot on his mind." His father looked at him. "Jack won the Spirit Award tonight. We're counting on him to handle it."

Jack wasn't sure who *we* was, nor what *it* was. Nor whether his father was lying, or finally telling the truth.

"Spirit, huh?" Misty said. "That's great!"

He hurried off to his new room, which had been designed as a large, walk-in closet—a long rod ran the length of it. Would his stepsisters sleep here too? He realized he'd left his duffle full of clothes in his mother's car. He slunk back into the living room to borrow a pair of his father's pajamas. Misty whispered something and tried to stifle a guttural laugh.

As Jack lay in bed, he imagined the speech the coach should have given: "This young man stuck it out. This young man gave it his all. This young man cheered when appropriate. Kept his mouth shut when appropriate. He smiled so hard his teeth ground into dust. He showered dutifully even when he had not broken a sweat. He always tucked his jersey in . . ." Jack heard a muffled moan through the wall, and another giggle. He started again, aloud this time, shouting to be heard, "This young man . . ."

Here's Looking at You(r) Kid

One day Becca took off her blue beret and never put it on again. She left it on a folding chair in the hallway outside our apartment, and it was the last I saw of her. Until today.

And her kid. In one of those snuggly baby carriers against her chest, sleeping, tiny head peeking out, tuft of dark hair. Her kid!

We stood in the CVS parking lot where the Ryan Theater used to be, reliably showing second-run double features until it CLOSED FOR REPAIRS until the end of time. I was going in for antacids and antianxiety meds. She was emerging with a square ton of disposable diapers. My dad was using Depends himself, but I bought those by the double ton out at the Costco near where I lived.

•••

"Holy shit," I said.

"Good to see you too," Becca said. Gaunt and slack and obviously exhausted. No wedding ring, I noticed—after twisting down to look at her hand beneath the handle on the shopping cart instead of immediately offering to help. "Immediately" as a concept was causing me some trouble, and thus I was on a quest for the perfect meds to help clarify that.

"I got a job," I said.

"Willie," she said, "It's been at least two years. I hope you've had at least one job." She paused and bent her neck toward her chest. "Say hello to Ava."

"Hi, Ava," I whispered, suddenly concerned about waking her. "Sally Redfern has a baby named Ava too."

"Good for her . . . No, fuck her," Becca said. "That stupid bitch."

"I go by Will now." Sally and Becca and I all had raw entanglements with each other. Now wasn't the time to lay them bare only to flunk our high school oral history final again. I looked at Ava, and at Becca looking at me. I wanted to touch that tuft of hair.

"Who's the lucky father?" I asked, poorly feigning nonchalance.

"Look, Willie, we're not going there." The baby slumped red and sweaty in the green corduroy carrier. Late July morning, starting to heat up, a rare cloudless day on Eight Mile Road. I started the day with a little bounce in my step, but was now quickly wilting back into my own daily slump.

"Will," I said. "Don't they make summer versions of those carrier things?"

"*Will*, ask your friend Sally. Salvation Army didn't have a summer version, asshole."

"You look tired. Want to get a refreshing something or other? We can catch up. Maybe I can hold the baby."

"Whoa," she said, shaking her head. Her cart full of diapers started drifting away, and we both grabbed it at the same time. Her hand was sweaty. "Don't you need to get your drugs first? What are you taking these days?"

"Me, I'm just here for vitamins," I said. I had my loyalty card on my key ring and some bonus bucks to use up. "You said 'first.'" I smiled. "As in, first get your stuff, then we'll catch up. Have you had iced coffee? That's what they call it—iced coffee. Like it's some great invention to throw in a few cubes."

Sally Redfern went to high school with us less than a quarter mile away from where we stood. Both of us did a weird little shuffle like shy square dancers in between the yellow lines of one of the many empty spaces in the lot. The old neighborhood was going to hell. My father did his grocery shopping in that enormous drugstore—it was close to home. Even he knew his driving was getting herky-jerky and wervy-swervy.

Becca hadn't answered the "father" question. I held my breath to keep from asking it again.

We were so close to the high school—I might've been able to fold one of those diapers into a mushy absorbent paper airplane and send it bouncing off the bulletproof front door. In the spring, one girl had hunted down another and stabbed her to death in the middle of geometry class. Even Sally Redfern hadn't done something that horrible. Sally grew out of her meanness, though Becca had a little scar on the back of her neck from Sally's rat-tailed comb. I used to kiss that scar.

"When I have a baby, I'm gonna name it B-va."

I got a reluctant half-grin out of her. "What are you doing, back in the old neighborhood?" she asked. We'd moved out of it together three-and-a-half years ago, renting an apartment out on the ragged fringe of the suburbs, out where the numbered mile roads ended and some small farms still stood on their last stubborn legs in between housing developments and strip malls with chain steakhouses and drinking establishments with high round stools to sit on at high round tables that forced you to slouch.

"You living with your mom?" I asked. Her mother still lived in the dark, stuffy house on Toepfer—what was actually 8 1/2 Mile Road, but that seemed too long and complicated for a street sign. I missed her mom, who, after her husband, Train-Wreck Teddy, drank himself to death, started working at the church food pantry and was now running the place. Going gangbusters, my own mother had told me when she was still alive and well enough to volunteer there herself. Becca's mother had a soft spot for charity cases like me. She made me grilled cheese sandwiches anytime night or day when I used to drop by their house, from when I was five years old to when Becca and I almost got married then broke up.

She stroked Ava's hair and did not look up. I took that as a yes. "Just checking on my dad," I said. "I'm still out in the boonies. Got myself a place in Trenton Mobile Home Estates. Working at Boss's Eatery in a strip mall off of 26 Mile. I don't go in till four."

"Why would anyone eat at a place called Boss's Eatery?" she asked.

"I don't eat there," I said. "I've moved up from busboy to waitstaff. Bright future, all that," I said.

"Mobile Home *Estates*." We both laughed.

"Sorry about your mom," Becca said. Our conversation was on tape-delay.

"Yeah," I said. "Yeah," I said again. "Everybody came to the funeral," I said.

"Not everybody," she said.

"Yeah," I said again.

"I loved your mom," she said. "I was busy having this one here."

Ava gurgled and stirred. I got a lump in my throat: my mom. Baby Ava. Lump, lump.

•••

I circled the cart as if guarding it from running away. Glad I had my new script in hand. I'd tried to cut back on the dosage, but the doctor doubled it instead. I had six more months on my dad's insurance. She had less, I suddenly realized. Her and Ava. Was the mystery man kicking in anything, or had he vamoosed like a weasel rat? I hated the anonymous motherfucker. I do-see-doed to try and get him out of my system.

"Ava Rose is her name." Rose, Becca's mother's name. We'd never talked about having kids in our two years living together, though perhaps we had when we were kids ourselves on the playground way back when.

"I quit drinking too," I said.

"Well, that's something," she said. "I gotta say, you still kind of look like you drink."

I wanted to ask what that meant, but I kind of knew. Unshaven, squinting up from beneath a greasy mesh ball cap. I took it off and pushed back my long stringy hair. The hat said MIA on it, white letters on red.

"You seeing anybody?" she asked.

"Nah," I quickly shook her off. "I've seen everybody already."

"Me too," she said, and sighed. I knew that was all she'd be saying on the subject, vis-à-vis the father.

...

While I was veering up and down the air-conditioned aisles in CVS, I worried Becca was just going to ditch me. My antacid bottles were buy-one-get-one free, so that's what I did. And, despite being frantic, I grabbed a greeting card on my way to the prescription counter. "Thinking of you," it said. I would save it. Send it to Becca someday. Neutral enough, true enough. The cashier, my old neighbor Mrs. Pollak, asked if I had any questions for the pharmacist. I just stared at her.

She'd dyed her hair an odd, lurid shade of orange ever since we were kids. On the streets, we'd called her "The Flame." We used to ring her doorbell then run away because she lived alone and had no kids. We picked on her, is the only way to say it.

"No, you don't have any questions, Willie. You never do. You have all the answers . . ."

"Will," I said. I almost said "Mrs. *Po*lack." We had time on our hands back then for cruelty and slurs. Maybe all that orange dye was messing with her head. Or my head. I gritted out an impatient smile.

The coupon machine spat out a handful, and she tossed them at me. "Your lucky day," she said, like she did every time. One of the sourest people in the world, but I'm sure we'd contributed to that. Our parents shunned her too. I ran out the door with the stream of coupons flapping in my hand. It was my lucky day: Becca's car was idling in the handicapped spot by the door waiting for me.

"The Orange . . ." I started to say.

". . . Flame," she said. "Yeah, I know. Still blazing away . . ."

"Why did we always pick on her?"

"Get in," she said. "I'll drive around to the other side."

"Want my coupons?" I asked.

"Sure," she said. "You too good for coupons?"

I looked at her like I looked at the Orange Flame.

"Yeah, yeah," she said. "The man who never met a coupon he didn't like. A motherfucking sucker for coupons . . . Mrs. Pollak's getting me in at CVS part-time."

"I guess we could've been a little nicer . . ."

"Yeah, and you, Wily Willy, you coulda been a contender. You coulda been a fucking Eagle Scout in the Troop of No Return."

I smiled. The Troop of No Return. She remembered everything. We had our built-in world of private jokes. Maybe someday I could tell some of them to Ava. Who was the damn father?

•••

She breastfed Ava in the booth at Big Boy's. I was being weird about it, working so hard not to look that I was getting a headache. I'd spent a lot of time with those breasts. Hell, I knew them before they started to grow. We used to run in the sprinkler in front of her house in our underpants.

I was swilling de-iced coffee, as most former drinkers did down at the meetings. I really, really wanted a smoke. Or to take a pill, but those drugstore prescription bags were made from some special rattling material. What was the purpose of that? And they stapled the bag shut too. Like they were giving you the pills but didn't really want you to take them.

Becca was drinking a big glass of ice water. Big Boy's was going under, due to the chubby Big Boy being stuck in checkered overalls forever, not getting with the times. Not like at Boss's Eatery where everybody dressed in black and slicked their hair back with goo from a big tub in the backroom.

Nobody bothered us in our far-corner booth. BB's coffee had never been good—both bitter and watery, with endless refills to keep you vaguely dissatisfied. I'm no connoisseur. I couldn't even spell the damn word. "Isn't this the Big Boy's you streaked through back in high school?" Becca asked. She damn well knew it was, so I didn't bother confirming. I was trying to remember how and why we broke up.

"Ava Rose," I said. "What a pretty name."

"Let's just take a nap here," she said, tilting her head back against the back of the vinyl banquette. "I'm just so tired. All the time, Willie." Her plaintive voice cut me with its butter knife of unguarded love. The booth became infused with the stuffy comfort of her parents' house or mine.

"Yeah, let's catch some zzzzz's. Fuck Sally Redfern," I said, thinking it would make her laugh.

She gave me her little grin-grimace that said *what am I going to do with you*, the grin that made me fall in love with her at least three and a half times over the years, ignoring the grimace.

But she didn't have anything to do with me anymore, and that made me a little sad sitting there killing time for the rest of my life. Ava's cheeks glistened with milk, her damp thin curly hair pasted to the side of her tiny head. When Becca switched Ava over to the other side, I got a glimpse of the tattoo of the small heart near where her real heart was, beneath her left breast. Once I wrote my initials in that heart with a magic marker while she pretended to sleep.

•••

I hadn't thought of her in a while, and I was feeling anxious about opening up that Mystery Spot again—upside-down door, balls rolling up hill, defying gravity. Had we outgrown the sameness of each other's skins like old clothes, patched and repatched, then discarded?

I had Becca's name tattooed on my left bicep. I'd kind of forgotten about that too, if you can imagine it. As a string bean, I never wore sleeveless shirts. I had a number of tattoos, but only one with a name on it. Not arty or ornate.

Just BECCA in block letters. I wish it was a little smaller. The "A" stuck out beneath some of my short-sleeved shirts. I got it on reckless rebound, the dramatic gesture to show how stupid in love with her I still was. Should I show it to her now, I wondered. Nah.

We all got a lot of tattoos back then, and some of the guys were still getting them. I knew I had my last tattoo. It's on my ass and says "Ha Ha"—if that's the best I can do, then it's time to put the ink away.

•••

Remaining alive is an accomplishment until it becomes a burden. I'd suggest you ask my mother about that if she were still around.

Good for her, *and* fuck her. Becca and I thought it was either/or when it was both. So many things were both as we sat in the large booth that seemed to be swallowing us. I wanted to be closer. My cold coffee. Her melted ice, tepid water. Baby Ava got what she deserved, warmth and nourishment.

What kept us alive in the time we spent together trying to kill ourselves, to make ugly corpses with our stupid tattoos and pale, wan druggy bodies?

•••

At Boss's Eatery, we specialized in nothing—the usual bar fare. We were a unique restaurant masquerading as part of a chain. In fact, customers sometimes asked, "Where are all the other Boss's?" Our food had the blandness of a chain, and the layout of the joint was equally nondescript.

Our boss, the owner Joe Boss (yes, really), had delusions of becoming the next Longhorn Outback or TGI Applebee's.

I don't want to make a big deal about the drinking and drugs. We never actually entered the death zone like some of our friends. When the Claw finally got strong enough, it picked them up and dropped them down the chute to Never Neverland.

That would be the name for my restaurant chain, Never Neverland, but I imagine it's copyrighted by some distant relative of Peter Pan's.

For us, self-destruction was a part-time job that kept us from getting full-time jobs. The job that kept the time clocks at bay while we stumbled through our early twenties as if no clocks existed anywhere.

•••

"You think we partied so much because we had no imagination?" Becca asked.

"I wouldn't go that far," I said. "I'd go farther."

"Can I tell you something?" she asked. And, uncharacteristically, she waited for an answer.

"Sure," I said. I was going to say something smart about how she never asked permission to say whatever she damn well wanted, but she looked so sweet with that child that I was getting all melty.

Though we'd never talked about having children, we had broached the subject of marriage on at least a few blurry nights. Why not? we asked each other. How would it be any different? What was the downside?

"Yeah, sure, what the hell," she said, as if she was talking to herself. "So, when Ava was a few months old, I laid her down for a nap in my old room. I was standing on the landing of my folks' house, you know, the spot where the sun shines through that weird round window . . . and I suddenly had this—this physical thing came over me, and I just wanted to fuck. Not fuck anybody, but you!"

"Of all people." I smiled. How many people in your life can talk about a spot in their childhood home and put you there instantly, feeling that sun?

"Of all people." She smiled back. "The feeling went away, of course."

"Of course."

"But not—not the memory. I kept wondering, why Willie? Why now? What's that asshole up to these days?"

"It gives me great pleasure to think about being part of one of your sexual fantasies."

"Oh, my fantasies are much better than that," she said. "We had too much reality together to make it a good one. It wasn't really a fantasy—more like this eerie haunting. Like I'd missed something, and it was circling back at me . . ." Ava lost the breast, and Becca reached down and helped her find it again. Like an old pro.

". . . Like a shark, circling. Like I was at my fertile peak after having Ava, and my body was telling me I should have another baby, a baby with you."

"Wow," I said. "That's weird. Though it's getting me kind of hot. Can we go over your ma's right now? That landing awaits us."

"I knew I shouldn't have told you," she said with an exaggerated groan. Exaggerated because she knew all along, given her hesitation, how I'd react. The bill for my coffee had been sitting on the table for at least half an hour, and I grabbed it. It was slightly stuck to what I was guessing was syrup from somebody's pancakes earlier that morning. As someone who wiped down a lot of tables, I'd developed a knack for identifying food fossils.

•••

Our breakup was predictable, looking back on it. We were immature and got on each other's nerves, particularly when we were either sober or drunk, which pretty much rules out any other time. Except when we slept. We were champions at sleeping together as a euphemism for sleeping together.

Becca got up and took Ava to the restroom to change her diaper.

I picked at the sticky piece of paper in the hardened syrup and pulled out a couple of dollars for the tip. Though I'd become a big tipper, considering my low wages, I dinged the girl a buck for the sticky residue. I calculated that our booth sat where the back of the Ryan once was, in the last rows where Becca and I used to make out through those long Saturday afternoons of forgettable second-run films.

•••

My father lived alone in the old house. I still kept some of my crap there, relying on the anchor of the old place for storage. Some overpriced band T-shirts, my old, scuffed Doc Martens from when they were a thing. Easier than moving boxes from apartment to apartment. Becca and I had split the kitchen stuff—the only thing we owned together in that furnished place.

She didn't ask for my new address or phone, but I didn't read much into it. I knew her address, and she still had the same phone. So did I. Though I'd learned to travel light, I carried the weight of my past around in my pocket. I had names in my contacts that were a complete mystery. And a surprising number of dead people in there. Like the junk I had at the old man's house, I just couldn't get rid of them.

"I lost one of our spoons," I said.

"I've still got all mine," she said. "Gonna need them soon," she said.

...

As we stood at the Big Boy's cash register, Becca handed me her child while she gathered some change from her bag, insisting on paying for my coffee. "Ava Rose," I said again, almost singing it.

"Better than B-va," Becca said. I hadn't held a baby in my arms before. Can you believe it? I keep thinking I must have held someone's baby, but when, when? Whose baby would I have held? I can't say the kid was smiling, but she wasn't crying like me.

I was going to mention this, but then I looked up at Becca, her arms already reaching out to me to give back everything that was hers.

Background Noise

We do not willingly / offer much to the creature world, a little food to amuse our loneliness.

—Jim Harrison

The TV was on. No one was watching it. My nephew Albert looked puzzled, having opened the door and let me in. His wife, Suzie—or Sooz, though I could not call her that, given the warmth and informal goodwill it implied—was on the phone, clearly telling somebody what-for. The nine-year-old twins, Bim and Jim, were chasing each other in a mad circle. Albert held up his hand. I thought he was going to shake mine, but he was giving an air stiff-arm to the kids that stopped them nearly quick enough to cause rug burns or sparks.

•••

My grandfather had insisted on leaving the TV on to keep his fat dog Ralph company while we took him to some family occasion at which his presence was required. Ralph had the benefit of a human dog's life. My grandfather cooked him pancakes and hamburgers in his ancient cast-iron frying pan. He never rinsed it out, so it always contained a toxic mix of burned food scraps and the yellow stink of old grease.

One day, stopping to check on him, I found the heavy pan on the floor tilted up against the fridge, and I figured out that my grandfather at age ninety-five finally could no longer lift the pan. He stood, head bowed, hands on hips, as I picked it up and put it back on the stove. I expected something from him—an explanation, some comment, I don't know what, really—but he remained silent, his lips trembling slightly with what was unspoken. The dog looked at me soberly. Whatever had been in the dropped pan, Ralph had taken care of. My grandfather walked into the living room, where he sunk into his ancient easy chair, leaning his head back against the stained antimacassar, which may have not been washed since my grandmother had died ten years earlier. He looked ready to join her. Ralph had dutifully followed him, plopping down at his feet with a heavy thud.

I thought about mopping the sticky floor. I thought about scrubbing the pan with steel wool, or taking a sander to it to erase the accumulated residue, trying to recondition it, but I just kept thinking about the watery eyes of my grandfather and the clear eyes of the dog. I wondered if Ralph had eaten his last pancake. I felt like the heavy thudded clang of that pan on the floor was a sign, and it was. Within a month, my grandfather was dead.

...

Albert, his great-grandson, took Ralph when my grandfather died. Albert slimmed him down, and the dog lived five more years. Maybe Ralph somehow had insisted that the TV be left on while he lived there, and it had just become the norm in that house. If he couldn't have pancakes, at least he could still listen to the shrill, exaggerated TV sounds trying to sell something, or to get you to laugh, or scare you, or whatever. But as Ralph would tell you if he wasn't a dog, you can't smell or eat TV, so I'm not sure how much the TV really did for him.

...

My grandfather fed Ralph whatever was available, so Ralph ate a lot of Meals on Wheels. The kindly volunteer driver, a grandmother herself, remarked that my grandfather had quite an appetite. Ralph, in turn, helped keep him alive, if only to get up and let him out and in a few times a day. Good boy, Ralph. Making it to ninety-five living on your own, quite an accomplishment for anyone. My own father wasn't going to make it that far.

•••

I hadn't been such a great-grandson or uncle. My sister, Jean, was Albert's mother. If I'd been the age I am now when my grandfather was dying, I might have been more sympathetic and caring. I had a softball game to play the night my mother called to say, "If you want to say goodbye to him, you'd better come now."

A playoff game. One of my teammates had begged off on his twenty-fifth wedding anniversary to be there. My grandfather, a big baseball fan who remembered Ty Cobb, would have wanted me to go to my game, I told my family. I've come to distrust anyone who claims to know what a dead person would have wanted. It's like pretending to know what a dog is thinking, which maybe I just did.

•••

Albert, Suzie, and the twins Bonnie and Jim. Bim was short for Bonnie somehow, and Jim, of course, for James. No one turned down the sound. At nine, the kids were still mostly polite, though disinterested—maybe they'd already written off their sober great-uncle who only made cameo appearances during the holidays.

I first sat on the couch, then quickly shifted over to the La-Z-Boy on the side to avoid the enormous glare of the TV screen. It was like they always had company—the people on the screen nearly as big as Bim and Jim. A lot of names end in "im"—I hope Bim doesn't marry a Tim and Jim marry a Kim.

"What are you watching?" I asked.

"Nothing special," Suzie said. Albert nodded as if I'd asked a question that did not deserve a reply. The kids ignored me, staring vacantly at the screen.

Cartoon Network, it appeared, and somebody needed to calm down and become human again. Maybe me.

I had never been in their house before. I lived seven hours away in deep, dark Indiana. I work in Elkhart, the RV capital of the world, at Jay Sport Camping Trailers. The Jay stands for nothing. The company founder thought it sounded sporty.

•••

I made small talk, waiting, until I realized that the TV was staying on.

"Uncle Carl, why are you here?" Suzie asked finally.

"Can someone please get me a glass of water?" I asked the people on TV.

"Bim, get your uncle some water," Suzie said. She squeezed the remote in her hand. One of the many.

"Hmmph," Bim said, not quite cute anymore, and stomped off into the kitchen, which had obviously been redone, as is the initiation rite for anyone living in this particular suburb. Some of my old friends from high school who lived nearby had shown me their kitchen islands and peninsulas. Suburban tropical.

•••

I drank my water. Cold, from one of those refrigerator water hookups that always break after a year or two.

"We're moving my dad into a home," I said. "Nobody can handle him anymore." The aides who came in twice a day to get him up and to put him to bed could no longer do either. Like Ralph, he was expanding into extra-large. His wheelchair, a double wide.

My father had paid the bills and let my grandfather live on his own as long as he could—longer than he could. No room at our family inn for the guy who never mentioned his other son, the one who died, who held it against my father that he'd been the one to live. Who never told the secret, even to those who already knew it.

Or son. I should have mentioned. I have not been a very good son. Why Indiana? When the car jobs dried up, a trailer job seemed like the next best thing. Indiana was flat like lower Michigan. Crossing the border was hallucinatory, except the hallucinations sped up in Michigan, as was the tradition of Michigan drivers, a slur in Indiana—"Michigan driver!" they shouted out their car windows at each other. While I don't want to get into my own complicated love life, I will say that in Elkhart I could be an Indiana driver without anyone tailgating me.

In any case, I'll be getting in line behind the old man on the lonely road to No Return before I know it, no matter what state I live in. I don't believe I'll meet Ralph there. *All Dogs Go to Heaven* was a cartoon that starred the voices of Bert Reynolds and Dom DeLuise, both deceased. Am I showing my age?

•••

My sister and I were planning to get our father a single room. If he ever stopped knowing who we were, we'd move him to a double. Or if his money ran out first. Then, we'd take what Medicare'd give us. He'd take.

"I love my father," I said. "But I can't lift him either."

"You're in Indiana," Albert said, looking at me over his glasses as if he did not believe me, sizing me up like an actuary.

"You could lift him, Al," I said. "Big guy like you."

"You're not suggesting," Suzie said.

"No, I'm not," I interrupted. Al sold life insurance. They'd started out in a little mom-and-pop branch in a strip mall and now had their own building near an exit off I-75. Suzie was Mom. I didn't even know life insurance was still a thing, though I understand it's kind of a tax shelter now. They'd tried to sell me some, but I wasn't buying.

"But we could use your pickup truck and help with the move. We've got to get him out of the house and into the home—isn't that ironical? Shouldn't it be out of the home and into the house?—and get rid of at least half his stuff. We'll have to sell the house. I'm using up vacation time to come up and do this. He's first on a waiting list."

The kids had disappeared. I had neglected to bring them bubble gum like I used to. Their parents hated bubble gum. I, who will never have grandkids, had to spoil somebody, and that's how my grandfather spoiled me, by giving me things my parents did not want me to have—soda pop, candy, potato chips, cheap plastic toys from the dime store—cowboys, Indians, soldiers. And how my grandfather spoiled Ralph—minus the plastic.

After Ralph died, Albert and Suzie did not get another dog. The kids didn't even know about Ralph, like we did not know my grandparents had another son—that my father had a brother who died of a burst appendix when he was in high school—until we were adults. "If we tell them about Ralph, they'll just want another dog," Suzie said in her Sooz voice. "No dog," Albert affirmed.

The kids might whine about getting another dog, but my father could not whine about getting another brother. The thick curtain of grief followed him and his parents around forever. My grandfather, quite frankly, did not seem to like my father at all. The more my father did for them, the less they liked him. After my grandmother died, my grandfather talked more to Ralph than he did my father.

"He's sitting over there now with that giant speaker next to his ear watching right-wing news shows and nodding. He can't even get up to make himself a sandwich anymore. He 'lost' the emergency help button we got him. The house smells worse than every nursing home your mother and I visited."

I looked at Albert's severe buzz cut. He was stroking his head like a Rott-weiler he was trying to calm down. Big house, successful career. Remodeled kitchen. Kudos to Albert. The kids probably had to climb a ladder to get into his pickup, which also sported bulked-up side panels, as if was guzzling steroids instead of gasoline. I probably shouldn't have made the right-wing crack.

I'd promised Jean I'd make this request in person. "He won't listen to me," she'd said. "He won't say no to you," she'd said. I'd never asked him for anything in my life, so I wasn't sure where she'd gotten such confidence. I could have gone on forever, just like the TV, trying to wear them down, but they really didn't care. Their twin nine-year-olds were screaming at each other from somewhere in the back of the house, where it sounded like another TV was blaring, part of their argument.

Suzie got up to check on the kids. I could hear her firm voice hammering down on them. Each kid was sent to their own room to cool down, but Suzie did not come back. She was probably in the bathroom sighing, waiting for me to leave. It was just me, Albert, and the TV. Albert juggled one of the remotes. He changed the channel to an obscure all-sports network: soccer players played volleyball with their feet. I'd seen it before. The novelty wears off.

My sister Jean had borne the brunt, but she knew my faults and did not seem to begrudge having to take on the role of primary caregiver. Brunt. That's a tough word. Begrudge. Growing up, I had spent a lot of nights in our tiny box of a house eating my dinner alone in the tiny kitchen that had never been remodeled, exiled by my father, who had no brother, but had a son.

...

"Give me a date," Albert said. "Give me a date, and I'll try to be there. Not with bells on, but . . ."

Bells on. He had added a lot of insurance salesmen quirks to his vocabulary, as if he'd learned English from a David Mamet character.

I do quality control on the trailers. I camp on Lake Michigan, on the tiny wedge of it that Indiana owns. Indiana Dunes—it's almost beautiful. I was close enough to sneeze in Elkhart and be heard in Michigan, but it was not Michigan. In self-imposed exile from the state I loved.

Why had I never asked my grandfather about his dead son? Why were we passing down silence from dog to dog?

To get to Chicago, I had to drive through Gary, Indiana, which, despite *The Music Man*, was better known as one of the top-ten armpits of America, one of the many little Detroits. All my compasses tilted back to Detroit, the original armpit. My father used to wrestle me into his armpit in a playfully violent way until I outgrew him.

•••

"I'll get you a date," I said, and stood. It almost sounded like a threat. I was living alone in Elkhart. Couldn't I find a way to move my father down there, or retire early and move back to the Motor City? I was fifty-five. Double nickel. A nickel for your thoughts. Hey, Dad, what's on TV?

I grabbed one of the remotes and pushed the *off* button, but nothing happened. "I'll get you a date."

•••

I spent the next day with my father, discarding family garbage and family treasures and deciding what clothes he might want to die in while he sat watching his TV, the giant speaker drowning out all chance for discussion. He had been the one to help everybody else die—his parents, his aunts, two cousins. Was he making up for not being able to help when his brother died? I hadn't asked him about my dead uncle either.

He'd handled all their paperwork and emptied all their houses. I'd just thrown out his neat folders of documentation. I had loaded up the garage with donations and trash and was getting ready to head out.

"Dad," I said, "can I get you anything?"

My father clicked his TV off and looked me in the eye. "Now, it's my turn" is all he said.

The Heart-Attack Bear

Every year at Christmas, a group of guys from our old football team at Eight Mile High got together for drinks at the Alibi. I looked forward to it—forty-five, divorced, I was more and more susceptible to "Glory Days" disease. When Sam, our old quarterback, called to tell me some cheerleaders got wind of our reunion and planned to join us that year, and would I mind, I said, "Damn right, I mind."

Nobody else's ex was one of those cheerleaders, if we don't count Sam's high-school flame, Patty—and Sam doesn't count her, so I guess we wouldn't. Both my ex-wife, Debbie, and my ex-sister-in-law, Debbie's twin, Ginger, were horning in on our annual get-together. Sam O'Brien, who spent half our high school years lusting after Ginger only to end up marrying and divorcing not one but two dancers from the Booby Trap, wanted to see how she'd held up over the years, regardless of my personal feelings. Sam wasn't the slick operator he'd imagined himself to be, and rather than starting out fresh with new people, he seemed intent on keeping connections with friends he'd lost touch with during his cocaine-cowboy years and his resulting stint in the county lock-up.

He had organized the first gathering five years ago, and saw himself as the mayor of the very small town of our old crew. When we were at Eight Mile, he'd organized a sophisticated alcohol-buying network that he later applied to cocaine, miscalculating the fact that "hey, those guys had guns and shit," but he never lost confidence in his ability to bring people together for his own benefit.

Sam and I were the only ones still keeping score on the original board while everyone else had constructed and discarded multiple scoreboards and were still building new ones: colleges, for those who went; careers, for those who have or had them; kids, and now grandkids. Using computer spreadsheets while Sam and I were still playing board games with spinners, pegs, and fake money. Pop-O-Matic Trouble was more our style. I'd torn down all those scoreboards in fits of rage or self-pity, like an angry kid upending the Monopoly board. In my head, I was stuck paying rent on Boardwalk and never quite passing go. Sam and I both fit in a box marked Other, and that was enough to keep us in touch.

"Damn right, I mind." The twins coming back to stick a pin in the Balloon Boy rejected by the Thanksgiving Day Parade—Detroit always has a big one, and Debbie and I loved to go to it, standing on a cold curb, giddy, stomping our feet to keep them warm, waiting for the bands and floats and, of course, Santa at the end. Since we never had kids, we never stopped believing, if that makes any sense.

After five years, the thought of seeing both Ginger and Debbie again sent me straight to the liquor cupboard above the fridge in our little house on Wilde Street that we bought from their Aunt Lil. When Debbie left, she moved into Ginger's place, then off to Ohio and parts unknown. I took down the Christmas whiskey and poured myself a stiff two fingers and tossed it back.

I wasn't much for whiskey. A beer guy from day one. Beer-drinking, ball-cap-wearing factory kid who had no business going to college—not even to play football—except I got caught up in the TV storyline that going to college would be my salvation.

I needed a beer chaser from the fridge to put out the fire. That whiskey—Seagram's Seven—could've been left over from our wedding twenty-five years ago. I always set those half-gallon bottles on the counter with mixers when Debbie and I had our holiday open house. After the party, I'd stick them right back up there until the next year. Then, everybody stopped having open houses at Christmas or any other time—couples having kids, getting divorced, or both. Or making new adult friends from work, or moving out to outer-burbs, or even out of state during one of the three recessions we've been through since our graduation.

When Sam, "Call-Me-Boomer," first suggested the Alibi reunion, everyone was on board—the dust had settled, but now it was turning to mud and we were sinking. Someone had put a death page on Facebook that listed our deceased classmates. Why not get together before our names made the list?

•••

Ginger found Sam/Boomer on Facebook, in the Alive section, and they started going back and forth about good old days. He boasted about organizing our annual Alibi get-together, and Ginger said, "Can I bring a group of girls along? I keep in touch with my cheerleaders."

"What am I gonna say?" Sam said to me, bragging about being her Friend as if that meant something besides a quick click. He lives near New York City. After getting out of prison early (model inmate who figured out how to work the system), he took community college classes down at Twelve Mile High and got an associate's in computers right when that stuff was taking off, and even an ex-con like him could get retraining funds. He ended up with a high-tech firm out east. Sam doesn't think about what our lives are like here during the rest of the year. He believes we're frozen in time, waiting for him to come back and unfreeze us every December.

"I said, 'Well, Big Bear's gonna be there,'" Sam paused, "and she said, 'Oh, Chris won't mind.'" I shook my head just imagining it—either her saying it or Sam making shit up. I started tumbling into speculation, wondering if maybe Ginger had set up Sam and Deb in some perverted lonely-hearts-club way. Was the husband of two topless dancers legitimate dating material for her sister?

"What about Patty?" I asked. "She should be invited."

"You think she wants to see me? I ruined her life, dude. I sent her a letter from prison, and I got one back from her husband threatening me if I ever said boo to her again . . . And you know she ain't talking to Ginger."

"But it's okay for Deb to come?"

•••

I arrived at the Alibi early as a strategic move, nervous as tables filled up around me. I'd guaranteed the hostess that at least twelve of us were showing up. Somebody'd have to leave a big tip for holding the table, and I was guessing that somebody would be me.

After one year of football on the frozen tundra of the UP at Michigan Tech (a hockey school), I dropped out and married Debbie, the "plain" twin. In middle school, Ginger blossomed into an exotic beauty with wicked curves, dazzling eyes, and the puffy lips of a teenaged movie star. She was well aware of those new assets, quickly abandoning us when the high school boys came sniffing around.

She had a thing for fast cars and the guys who drove them—not football players driving their father's station wagons—but she also demanded the attention and flattery that my teammates eagerly provided, lurking around her locker as if they had a chance.

Tech was a longer drive from Detroit than New York City. How far away can it be, I thought, if it's in Michigan? Five hundred and fifty miles, it turns out. I also didn't understand that their fire hydrants had flag poles in order to help find them under ten feet of snow. I must not have been paying attention in our required Michigan history course—Mr. Rash, the football and wrestling coach, taught it. I guessed *Pere Marquette* when I didn't know the answer, and it was right often enough to get me through. Good old Coach Rash, with his golden toupee and rooster strut. He would have been a great villain on studio wrestling.

•••

Sam and I, a package deal coach set up with the Tech coach, roomed together that one year. I spent many nights at their Alibi—doesn't every town have at least one?—when I should've been studying, the snow piling up above the bar's thick windows. I felt like an action figure manipulated by a snowman kid in some futuristic ice-age computer game, if that makes any sense. If that makes any sense. My brother, Ken, tells me I say that too much. That I should stop qualifying everything.

I left Sam at Tech. He stayed two more years and went on to become president of his fraternity. He wrecked his car drunk-driving into one of those giant snow banks and came out unscathed. But he dropped out too after having his knee wrecked by a massive defensive lineman from Northern Minnesota and developing a fondness for painkillers along with a fondness for the money he'd made selling drugs back home over the summer.

"Remember that snow, dude?" he asks every time we talk because I had been there long enough to see it. No one else we knew had ventured that far north.

•••

The Eight Mile Bears' mascot, Mr. Wallace, the alcoholic shop teacher, donned an old, matted bear costume for pep rallies and football games. In his classic routine, he'd collapse after an energetic chorus-line dance with the cheerleaders, then they'd gather around to revive him. The crowd always roared when he finally stood up. Mr. Wallace hammed it up big time. Everybody called him the Heart-Attack Bear. The cheerleaders hated him, his boozy sweat oozing its stench through the costume while he tried to grope them—he could get away with anything while wearing that costume.

Inevitably, he did have a heart attack—alone at his house, shoveling snow, not in front of the adoring or mocking fans. The bear costume was buried with him, and no one was ever the Heart-Attack Bear again, though I inherited the name.

I can't remember who first called me "Heart-Attack Bear," though I know it was after I returned from Tech and gained a lot of weight. Nobody seemed to have any trouble calling me that to my face. It was said, I believe, with a certain affection, with a pat on the shoulder, "Hey, it's the Heart-Attack Bear!"

Over time, my friends cut it to Bear, and I accepted the shortened version, using it to identify myself on the phone: "Hey, Bear here, what's up?" At least they didn't shorten it to Heart Attack. Not everybody had a nickname. Despite Sam wanting us to call him Boomer, it never stuck. I don't know what they called him in prison.

...

I sat, shoulders hunched, belly pressed against the table, sweating down the insides of the puffy winter coat I refused to take off. The Alibi's a sports bar, like most big suburban joints, stuffed with TVs playing whatever sport was in season. Conveniently located right off I-96, and we could corral a big table, and they didn't mind us lingering, nursing our beers because we all had the drive home ahead of us. Its regulars clustered around the bar, ignored the holiday riff-raff behind them at the tables in the center of that loud, enormous room.

Between Christmas and New Year's, there's at least one bowl game a day. I glanced at the soundless TVs with closed captions—most of them showing the same game. Some hyphenated corporate-sponsored game. A couple of 6–5 teams from the South—somebody running the old wishbone formation. If you've got the right personnel, it still works. They were lighting up the scoreboard—the slick QB pitching out or keeping it on sweep after sweep, always guessing right—but around that scoreboard you could see the half-empty stadium.

•••

Frank and Tony were bringing their wives, the Lewinski twins, from two grades behind us in school. They looked a lot more alike than Ginger and Debbie—they could even fool the teachers. Of course, Frank and Tony could tell them apart, and the four of them appeared to be living happily ever after, neighbors out in the manicured flatness of Rochester Hills, where they have cookouts together.

We hadn't had an official reunion since year five, and that didn't really count—we weren't much different at that point. No one was labeled a complete failure yet. Those guys go to their wives' reunions, hanging with the younger crowd, though to be honest, at our age, two years is nothing—not like the ten years Ginger's first husband Gino, a rich Italian restaurant owner, had on her. Gino of the Gold Chains, Deb and I called him. A trophy wife at first, but Ginger wasn't happy getting all dusty in the attic, so she dumped him. And next thing I know, Deb dumped me, even though we're the same age.

•••

The table stuck to my elbows when I leaned forward. I caught the waitress's eye and made a wiping motion with my hand, but she just smiled and kept moving past. "What penalty is that a signal for?" she asked when she finally made it over to me. A cute young girl weighed down by thick mascara—age wise, she could've been the love child of me and Deb, the one we never had, the one we sent over Niagara Falls in a barrel.

"Sorry—can you wipe down this table?"

"While I'm here, can I take your order?" she asked.

It sounded like she said "odor"—she had a small speech defect. I tune in to those things. In remedial speech class, we bonded like the football team, leaving our regular classes together to visit the therapist, but as soon as someone corrected their defect, they were gone, denying they ever knew us. Repeat after me: shame was the name of the game. We had no cheerleaders, no letter jackets. No one to fudge our stats. The last time I stuttered was when we signed the divorce papers.

Sam used to stick up for me when I got teased about my stutter, but now he won't ease up about my weight. He takes it personally, like I'm an uncomfortable reality check on the football stories he's embellished over the years. Brother Ken gets on me about my weight too—my business partner in our unequal family business. He makes all the decisions, and it's his business to be in my business.

"Just water for now, please," I said.

"Popcorn too," I added as she walked away. The Alibi provides baskets of fresh, salty popcorn. I've always been a big snacker, nervous for my hands to do something besides fold into good behavior. My pulse throbbed in my ears. My fingers and toes numbed. I kept taking deep breaths, jerking my eyes toward the door every time it thumped open—large, happy groups of family and friends crowding in. The nearest TV was airing the cartoonish spectacle of professional wrestling. I lettered in wrestling and made third-team all-state, but no one came to our meets. Nothing like the packed stands at football games.

Wrestling might seem more primitive than football, but it's more controlled, at least in high school. All Coach Rash could do was shake his long mane of blond hair and bluster at the referee from the edge of the mat—no play calling, no substitutions. Just two wrestlers, with the referee giving points: Takedown. Escape. Reversal. Near fall. Riding time. Nowhere to hide, exposed in your wrestling singlet. The drama of a referee thumping his palm against the mat to indicate a fall. Nothing in my life has been that clear except Debbie getting pregnant.

•••

I have a hard belly, like a large boulder—impossible to lose, impossible to forget every time I stretched a shirt on over it. A constant shame, like I'm in speech class again, but I can't stop babbling—no break, no silence. Sometimes in the shower, I punch the boulder to see if I feel anything in my fist, or in my stomach.

In public, I'm invisible. People rarely look at me when we talk, though I've come to appreciate that. Today, the girls were coming, and the sweat was biblical. A fat, balding middle-aged man. No woman thinking, "I'd hit on that," like we did in high school, casually rating girls as they passed in the halls, half-serious, half-joking, half-oblivious, imagining any girls would have us at all.

•••

While Ginger evolved into an exotic interplanetary species like the Ginger of *Gilligan's Island* fame, Debbie remained simple and pretty in the Mary Ann kind of way my mother and others admired—more of a tomboy, not interested in glamming it up. Her biggest asset was a hearty laugh that penetrated all surfaces, all artifice. In other words, just the kind of woman for a shy, lunky, lineman.

I'm not big on the names of flowers, but Ginger was definitely a bold, expensive rose with sharp thorns. Debbie was more like the pot of reliable marigolds you bought on the side of the road on the way to Mother's Day dinner. I was happy to have her sweet, simple beauty by my side, year after year. She wouldn't wilt in hot weather. I hadn't counted on the fact of them being twins, the complicated connections beyond appearance.

•••

The barmaid brought a wet rag and my water. I ordered a couple of pitchers of Molson's, which they'd always had on tap, to assert my confidence that others were on their way.

"Nope," she said. They were going with microbrews now. She listed the IPAs and wheat beers and who knows what else, with names like Devil's Aardvark or some other nonsense.

"You got any *regular* beer?" I asked.

"Miller Lite," she said, and that's what I ordered.

•••

Sam barged in through the thick, steel door. He saw me sitting alone and hesitated, checking his watch. He glanced around nervously like there might be some mistake, perhaps hoping others were hiding somewhere, ready to jump out and surprise ol' Boomer, the mayor of Tinytown. Eventually, he acknowledged my wave and came over.

Sam once told me he counted all the girls he'd had sex with to help him sleep at night. He didn't remember all their names, so he'd refer to them as "the girl at Junior's party," "the girl on the speedboat," and on and on. He looked at me and laughed. "What's your number, Big Bear?"

After Debbie left, I made a list of things in my life I hadn't counted on—it started as self-pity, but as the list grew, it turned into a comfort to recite at night, like counting sheep, a pile-up of sheep on top of me, though I didn't even have the ball.

"I was never good at keeping track," I said.

"You weren't good at something," he said, and he gave me this look that made me suddenly wonder if he had slept with Debbie. He always talked like he had a canary in his mouth, but that look—something honest about it shook my smile into a shiver—like he'd pulled off a mask and revealed a face full of pity and disdain.

"Where's everybody?" He took out his phone and stared at the screen, then slipped it back into a case on his belt like a gunslinger eager for a shootout.

•••

Debbie and I had many family cookouts during our marriage. If they were taking odds back in high school on who'd still be together, we would've topped the charts. When Ginger showed up to our barbeques, she was usually hungover, slouched alone in a folding chair in her sunglasses like a movie star bored by ordinary life, petulant that no one recognized her. I don't remember Gino ever coming—the restaurant, a convenient excuse, with the implicit understanding that he didn't have to come to any family event. He gave Ginger all the money she wanted and, in exchange, got a free pass. Debbie and I were like concerned parents, like the seniors setting a good example for the freshmen, except everyone was bored by our example.

•••

"Did you ever break a rib?" I asked Sam as we sat at the long, empty table. He should have sat across from me, not next to me—I was reading motives into everything, on sensory overload after a year frozen in place.

"Nah," he said, "After all, I had you blocking for me, Big Bear!" And he clapped me on the back. I had in fact kept him from getting planted in the middle of the field on numerous occasions, his all-conference left tackle, pulling on sweeps down the sidelines—what a rush, just picking off those guys coming at Sam like bugs and I was a windshield.

"See," I said, carefully oiling myself up like the Tin Man, "loving Debbie was like a broken rib—I couldn't breathe without hurting after she left. If I inhaled too deep, I got this pain right here." I gestured toward my heart. "The pain's still there. I'm laying in bed by myself, feeling her in my ribcage, pounding on those ribs, and . . ."

"You're making me hungry talking about ribs, man," he tried to joke. I bit my lip and stared into my beer.

"Look, Deb's not coming," he said finally. "Ginger texted me. You and your damn ribs can relax. You sure you're not having a heart attack or something, Heart-Attack Bear?"

I took a long swallow of beer, trying to process what he'd told me. *Not coming.* I carefully set down my glass.

"That's what I'm telling you, Sam, I had a heart attack, and that's why I've never loved nobody else. I wish I had, but . . ."

"I always tell you this, but . . ." he started.

"'. . . Lose some weight,'" I finished.

"Something tells me she's not laying home by herself thinking about ribs. Not with a sister like Ginger."

"I'm not interested in what . . . you think . . . she's thinking," I said. "If you still lived here . . ." I said. I wanted to ask when was the last time he'd seen either of them. I took another long swallow to drown my slight stammer.

"We'd still only see each other once a year."

"I think that's all we could stand, but . . ."

"We'd still finish each other's sentences. What's that credit card commercial say?"

"Priceless. They say it's priceless."

"Did we have this same conversation last year?"

"Weren't you paying attention? We have the same conversation every year."

"Maybe there's some topics we haven't hit on. Check your list." We sunk into sullen silence.

"Remember that snow, dude?"

We both laughed.

•••

"Look who's coming to save the day," Sam shouted, spotting the rescue ship. "No wonder those guys never bring their wives—they still look eighteen."

Frank and Tony came in with Penny and Jenny. The twins didn't seem to recognize me as they strode toward us—like models strutting down the runway, if we're to believe Sam, and in this case, I'll go along with him. He'd quickly slicked his hair back like he's always done, like he'll do while waiting in line at death's door. *Do I look alright?* he'll be asking. And the Grim Reaper's assistant will stand there rolling his eyes: *Reaper don't care what you look like. He's been waiting for you, 'Boomer.' Everyone in hell will call you that!*

"There they are," Frank said, motioning to me and Sam.

"Chris Hawk—the Heart-Attack Bear!" Jenny shouted, finally, as if she was a quiz-show contestant solving the puzzle. The four of them gracefully slid across the long table from us. It seemed odd, like Sam and I were suddenly in for questioning. They all wore scarves around their necks and nice leather coats—not the studded black jackets tough guys wear. They looked like middle-aged models. I'd buy whatever they were selling to look that good again, though as Dr. Ravich tells me every year, being healthy isn't something you can buy your way into. It doesn't take bribes.

•••

"What's this watery stuff?" Tony asked, taking a tentative sip, then grimacing.

"Lite," I shrugged. "No more Molson's."

"Expand your horizons, Bear." Frank reached across to cup my neck. "Try some of the fancy shit. I saw one of your trucks the other day. Business good?"

I smiled. "Heating. Cooling. Everybody needs it." Ordering light beer—a joke on myself—but at least it wasn't some hoppy crap. I was against trends of all sorts. I was trending anti-trend.

•••

Going away to Tech was a huge deal when even going down the road fifteen minutes to Wayne State was considered a dubious move. The car plants were even closer and offered lifetime (or so we thought) job security, good pay, and bennies up the wazoo.

Our old school still sat exposed on Eight Mile Road. I remember the large glass windows facing traffic, rattling as the semis passed, though they were all boarded up now, just like a lot of the factories. The downturns blew some of us across state lines, but most came back. Some guys never left and ended up moving back into their parents' houses after they died. At least two developers had pulled out of redeveloping the old school site. Either the dreams were too big, or too small.

When I quit Tech and came home, those who noticed seemed kind of relieved. In our neighborhood, nobody really trusted the idea of college and where that could take you: away, away. Then, I was just like everybody else—only worse, because I'd briefly pretended to be the exception to the norm that after high school, you started in at the factory and stopped doing anything you'd want to tell stories about later. You had your high school stories, and you'd be telling them until you died. Springsteen's "Glory Days" sums it up. Some of the guys think "The Boss" is fake, but if he is, he's a good fake. Besides, if he worked the line, he'd never have had the time to write all those songs. My "Glory Days" were with Debbie. By the time we graduated, the whole school knew us as a couple, one unit (we didn't have a cute name like "Brangelina," though that one didn't work out so good either). Only Ginger could have pulled off some kind of combo like that at Eight Mile, but the bright lights of her name dimmed the bravado of even the biggest men on campus.

I did work the line for a few years. Ken, a guy with ambition, and, luckily, some heart, took me on in his heating and cooling business. He knew I could be trusted, which counts a lot in a small operation like his. For better or worse, as he says. If that makes any sense, I say.

•••

Ken ran a hand through his spikey silver hair and spat in a puddle on the cracked concrete outside Mankowitz's Funeral Home. Our buddy from next door in the old neighborhood—a guy we called "The Dude," due to his attachment to an old fedora his runaway father left behind—had gotten shot one night while taking out the garbage.

"What a way to go," I said.

Ken looked at me and spat again. "You could be right behind him," he said. A championship spitter from way back—for Ken it was punctuation. I could never master spitting. Like the "s" sound I got stuck on when I stuttered, extending it into a leaking tire. Ken's spits were periods. Mine were commas.

I told him about the girls' plan to invade our reunion.

"You sound like you're still eighteen. Get over it, brother. We're probably gonna die soon, just like The Dude. Nobody will have to shoot us, given our family death chart, and then who's gonna give a shit about high school? Look at you." He pointed one of his greasy stub-fingers, then grabbed a handful of my belly and squeezed. I pulled away. He gave me a little shove. Our dad kicked off at fifty-three from a heart attack.

"It's 'depth chart,'" I said, "not death. They're my friends, not scouts for *America's Next Hot Model.*"

"You watching that shit?"

"They're cool, but . . ."

"You're worried about seeing Deb. I bet she can't squeeze into her old uniform either. Nobody can. And why should they? When's the last time you had a date?"

"It's all on computers now, that's what I hear."

"Then get a fucking computer. Hell, use the one in the office."

•••

Ginger probably believes she looks after Debbie like Ken looks after me, but convincing your sister to leave her husband just because he put on a few pounds and watches too much TV—just because you left your own husband and want some company—doesn't qualify as "looking after." Sure, we had problems, but I never hurt her or cheated on her.

I always called her "Debbie's evil twin" as a half joke. Deb—Debbie—was happy to be part of Ginger's entourage. In high school, they shared a summer job at the A&W across from the school on Eight Mile. They shared a car, this Dodge Dart with a push-button transmission. I thought those push buttons disappeared a long time ago, but my new truck, a Dodge Ram, has a transmission knob like that Dart. It doesn't take much to remind me of Debbie and our life together in the little house on Wilde. Just three rooms, one bath, and it shrunk even further as we filled it with our lives. For at least the first fifteen of our years together, we were happy.

We never did drugs, never had kids, never bought stock—and we never went to Niagara Falls. Though Debbie showed her parents a postcard as proof—you can get a Niagara Falls postcard in a lot of places—she never went, with or without me. Our trip to "Niagara Falls" was cover for an abortion in Windsor, Ontario—nobody's idea of a honeymoon site, not even for Detroiters, whose standards are pretty low. She had the abortion so I could go to college. Make something of myself.

Everyone wondered why we never had kids. Especially Mr. and Mrs. Romano. No grandchildren coming from Ginger, and just what the hell was our problem?

•••

I went to college to play football—I didn't put much value on the free education. I missed Debbie too much. My first love, and I'd never been away from home that long before or since. I called her "Deb" until she left me. Now, I try to add that extra syllable, stretching it into something more formal. Sometimes I forget. Not "Deborah" though—none of us knew any Deborahs. Deborahs lived out in nice suburbs like Birmingham and all the Woods and Pointes where we made our money installing AC units and new furnaces, carefully covering the shiny hardwood floors and lush oriental rugs before we stepped on them with our work boots.

•••

At Tech, everyone on the team had been a star at their own high schools. Despite being too small or slow for Division I, a lot of them were still bigger and faster than me, and I realized I'd be warming up those frozen benches on the sidelines for the next four years.

At Eight Mile, we had our scaled-down versions of most things, including the definition of "big." Everybody at school thought I was big, but they added fifteen pounds onto my listed weight to make me seem bigger. The coaches at Tech wanted me to add weight to play in college, which I did, acquiring habits that resulted in me waving at 250 pounds in the rearview mirror as I passed. After dropping out, I still ate like a football player. And after Debbie left, I ballooned into a parade float of that cartoon character, the Heart-Attack Bear. I've got one fake knee now, with another on the way from holding up that weight.

···

How can I justify putting my health at risk? It's just who I am. That sounds lame. Maybe I should go back to stuttering. It's not hereditary, not the glands. Ask mean, lean Ken, hands on his hips, standing behind me with his glowering grin. Besides Ken, nobody I see in my daily life knew me back when I was jacked. At least I quit smoking, though that gained me another fifteen.

Once a year in Dr. Ravich's office, sitting on the exam table, my globe of fat exposed, I take it from him, and once a year at the Alibi, I take it from Sam, licking my wounds with old stories. My old teammates are so used to the big me *they'd* be having heart attacks if I showed up at my old weight.

···

Debbie left me the week after she complained that her underwear smelled like potato chips. I thought she was joking—like, "Chris, how could that happen?" I told Ken, and he laughed. "Brother," he said, putting a hand on my shoulder, "you're too much." It was like I'd been caught cheating with the Better Made Potato Chip Maid.

I'd been snacking while folding laundry in the living room and watching the Lions lose another game. Could've been any year, since they haven't won anything in over sixty, but it happened to be their last season in the Silverdome, 2001, when they lost their first twelve games before they finally beat the Vikings.

Debbie told Ginger in one of their "you're not going to believe what Chris did" conversations—I heard it over the phone, then Debbie lowered her voice and slid shut the pocket door between the kitchen and living room.

Ginger had just left Gino, and Debbie was having lots of phone calls and coffee dates with Ginger, who'd been working at Gino's restaurant (named Gino's—classic Italian food, pretty tasty) so suddenly she's got a lot of extra time. She asks Debbie, "How can you stand it? You have to leave him. He's pulling you down. We're still young enough to start over. We deserve it." At least that's what got passed down to me by Debbie on her way out the door.

"Potato chips in my underwear" became her refrain line and answer to all of my "whys." Then suddenly she's in Ohio living with some guy named Kyle. Though she left Ohio Kyle pretty quick. She and Ginger were having a making-up-for-lost-time contest for ex-cheerleaders. Debbie'd never had sex with anyone else, and neither had I. We were virgins at sleeping around, if that makes any sense. If life was a carnival, then suddenly I was working the dunk tank while Deb worked the kissing booth.

I'm collapsing time a little bit, but the Silverdome lost the Lions and I lost Debbie, neither of us living up to expectations. They finally tore down the dome. I bought one of the old seats, though it's a tight squeeze.

•••

For Deb, it was like the door on life slammed too fast, before she'd seen everything she wanted to. Things she didn't even know she'd wanted to see—with Ginger on the other side of the door calling *come in* with her sweet, syrupy voice. Ginger sounded like one of those old 800-number sex-line voices—sweet for a price.

•••

"Think, think," Dick Rash (his name, no kidding) would tell me, smacking my helmet. He always said I needed to be better at seeing the whole field, anticipating, but all I could see was the guy in front of me I had to block or tackle. He'd called in a favor for me with the coach up at Tech. When he saw me back in town, he smacked my helmetless head, "You poor sucker. You've got your whole life to fall in love—you just get one shot at football."

•••

I often spent evenings in the Romano's living room watching TV with Deb and her parents, or sometimes alone with Deb, quietly kissing on the overstuffed sectional on Saturday nights when her parents were out bowling in their mixed doubles league.

I'd tell Ginger: "be home by midnight," or "stay out of trouble," or "come home when the streetlights come on," or "be careful with the boys." Variations on the same joke—that I was her father. Ron Romano, their real dad, never told her anything as she went out the door. Ron, the invisible man in his La-Z-Boy with beer and cigarettes, watching the news, then "To Tell the Truth," then "Mannix," "Baretta," all the detective shows. "Colombo" was his favorite, though he himself was never curious. When I came back from Tech, Ron acted like I'd never left. No judgment, no criticism, no acknowledgment.

•••

Ginger flitted in and out past us in front of the TV, in various stages of dress, or undress, getting ready to go out or ready to crash. She had no idle switch. Ginger never brought anyone inside their house. When boys arrived, her parents got quick introductions in the driveway, if that, but they accepted it from the glamorous one. I was the plain guy with their plain daughter.

•••

One night, Ginger came into the living room wearing only an extra-large Eight Mile High football T-shirt and sat on the La-Z-Boy across from me. Anyone would've given her the shirt off their backs, so I'm not sure whose it was. Deb was out of the room—maybe talking on the phone or fixing us a snack. I was a fixture in the house by then, so nobody felt compelled to host me.

Fully reclined, Ginger slowly spread her legs so that I could see right up the T-shirt. She put her front teeth on top of her bottom lip—this incredibly sexy pout like she was holding something in that she wanted to let out. "Better than TV, huh Chris?" she said quietly.

I felt my face—my entire body—flare up. Then Debbie came into the room. "Chris, are you alright? What have you two been doing in here?"

"He farted," Ginger laughed.

• • •

Penny'd had breast cancer, Sam told me, and now she looked more like an older sister than a twin. I caught her staring at me strangely, maybe hoping to see my reaction when Debbie came in—a little fuel injection for the dull engine of our nostalgia. A long afternoon of remember-whens at the bar doesn't make for much, but that was all we had.

• • •

Ginger dated Carl Mitchell—the senior quarterback our freshman year—for a few months, then quickly moved on. Mr. Chubbs, a history teacher, snuck around with her off and on. She was deliberate in her choices. When Debbie tried to explain what was behind those choices, I just scratched my head. I kept that secret, though my face burned when I passed Chubbs in the hallway as if it was me doing something shameful.

• • •

When I heard Coach Rash was retiring, I knew I had to see a game that fall. He helped me get that scholarship to the tundra, thinking it was what I needed—get away, see the world, or at least Northern Michigan. Late one Friday afternoon, I was working in the old neighborhood and noticed the lights on at the field. Football weather—clear, a slight bite in the air. I grabbed a burger at Big Boys and headed over.

• • •

Looking over the program, I noticed some old teammates had kids playing for coach—man, I would've loved that.

The other guys at the Alibi commiserated about their kids—pride hidden behind complaints. Kids pulling new versions of old pranks, aided by computers and smart phones. Our old rival, Center Line High, had recently been in the news—kids sexting pictures of each other's junk.

"Yeah, like we wouldn't have done the same thing," Tony said.

"Computers make things too fast," I said. "When you're young, there's something missing in your brain—you pull this shit without thinking—now, there's no taking it back. It's all out there." I waited for a response, but nobody wanted to talk about putting it all out there.

"Sometimes I get in trouble for clicking *send* on emails at work," Jenny finally said. She had an associate's degree and worked at Mercy Hospital further down Eight Mile from the school. "I just can't resist telling off those know-it-all doctors."

"But you're not sending them pictures of your boobs," I said. I wasn't used to mixed company at the Alibi—that's my alibi. I'd forgotten Penny's cancer.

"Nice one, wise guy," Tony kicked me under the table when Penny and Jen headed off to the bathroom.

"I didn't know," I said, though I did.

"Dumbfuck, you never knew. Ever," Frank said. "Look at you," he said, as if that explained everything.

•••

I plunked down on one of the cold metal benches in the bleachers, A young couple down the row glanced over. I nodded, imagining I looked like a college scout—an old player, a sharp observer of the game. I got out my pen to doodle on the roster, but then I looked down at my work jacket: Hawk Brothers H&C, and my name stitched over the breast pocket.

Hawk Brothers H&C. Four trucks, eight employees, and a stable list of customers. Ken's married with three kids. His son Robbie works with us on weekends and during the summer. I wonder sometimes if Ken's grooming him to replace me: Hawk & Son.

Number 12, the Eight Mile quarterback, looked good in warm-ups. Crisp spirals, good footwork, but once the game started and he felt the pressure of the rush, he got happy feet, dancing around, tossing off-balance passes into the dirt or over the heads of his receivers. "Plant your feet," I stood and shouted. The young couple glared at me.

•••

Right before halftime, Debbie and Ginger showed up with their cousin Carla, who lived near Center Line and had a kid on their roster. Maybe Deb and Ginger had switched sides for the second half, just like they had in life, leaving me and Gino holding our pompoms in the parking lot. I should've contacted him after the twins left us. We could've talked about our own second halves.

Shame—the only word for it, though I've been throwing that flag for too long. They walked up the steps just as the crowd began stirring for halftime. Trapped in my front-row seat, I lowered my head, but picked it up too quickly and met Debbie's eyes right when she passed. She looked away, then kept going. Shock—maybe horror—on her face. All our years together packed into that look. I didn't tell anyone I saw her, not even Ken.

The crowd jostled them forward. They stopped in the middle of the bleachers, leaning against the railing, chanting with the cheerleaders, pumping fists. The cheers hadn't changed. The uniforms either—blue and gold skirts, blue sweaters, yellow megaphones. Some in the crowd hooted, and Ginger turned toward them with her open-mouthed smile, Debbie nervous and excited beside her.

I had to sit out one game senior year—my left knee, the one I ended up having replaced. I couldn't put pressure on it. Our trainer's answer to any injury was to put stinky green slime on it and send us back in. My knee buckled when I tried to loosen up, and I had no choice but to sit. I usually only got to check out the cheerleaders at pep rallies, but I was able to turn around that night and watch Debbie and Ginger, the Lewinski twins, and all the others spread out on the cinder track in front of the bleachers. I sat at an angle so I could both watch the game and watch the love of my life and her sister, jumping, shouting, doing flips, feeding off the crowd.

They seemed just as happy all these years later. Maybe they were hooked on high school like me. It had its claws into us, and we had nothing to pry them off, to replace them with something equally vibrant, sexy, alive.

...

Six other couples eventually arrived, plus another guy, Junior, flying solo, his wife begging off to babysit their first grandchild. Most of us weren't afternoon drinkers, and after switching to the strong microbrews, everyone seemed sleepy and slow. In the crowded bar, sweat gathered, leaking down my sides like it never did when it was just the guys.

Ginger made a grand entrance just as we were dulling down. She wore as much makeup as our waitress, but hers was artful and glamorous, overdone for the stage she imagined herself on. Her hair blew out into wild waves. Spikes of fake fur stuck out from her black jacket, a coat that'd been electroshocked. High-heel boots. Tight jeans. Despite Ken's belief, she would have fit any old uniform, though she had a gaunt tightness to her, a pressure inside ready to burst. Still, she turned heads.

Everyone stood. "Where's Debbie?" Tony asked quickly, glancing at me. While I don't imagine anyone thought we'd have this big Hollywood heartwarming reunion, to be honest, part of me had been hoping for just that.

"Debbie's got the Christmas flu. She said to say hi to all you guys." Ginger paused. She put her hand softly on my shoulder. "Particularly to you, Chris," she said, kissing me on the cheek. "She said to give you some tongue, but . . ." Everyone laughed, and I blushed, grateful for Ginger quickly defusing the awkward situation—though Debbie didn't like French kissing all that much.

Ginger looked at Frank and Tony, the twins—then at the empty space on my side of the table. She slipped around next to me.

•••

I tried to catch Coach Rash's eye, but his eye was on the field, as always. I waved to him once when he glanced back at the stands, but I could have been anyone waving to anyone.

My fallback position in life has always been to do nothing, so after the game—a Bears victory—I snuck out to the parking lot to sit in my truck and keep an eye out for Debbie and for coach, but in the rush of cars starting up, turning on their lights, backing out, I did not see either of them. *Coach, coach, put me in*, I would've said.

•••

"Remember Mr. Wallace?" Frank asked.

"Man, could that guy put it away. Just like our guy here. What suit we going to bury you in?" Tony said, still mad about my stupid remark to Penny. Short, fast, with a little guy's temper—he reached across the table toward me in a threatening gesture, half-playful, but serious enough for Frank to pull him back in his seat. I slumped down into my puffy jacket—my bear suit.

•••

"We saw you at the Eight Mile game," Ginger said, leaning into me, and I felt her warm soft breath against my ear. She patted my thick thigh under the table. "Oh, Chris, Chris," she said. Then she out-and-out punched my leg, in enthusiasm, anger, or both—I wasn't sure. Too late to ask as she launched herself into the Ginger zone, surrounded by an audience that envied her reckless life, the lurid mascara, the loud pop of her old gum.

Since we had been related for so many years, we could fill the rest of the afternoon with catching up, circling around those couple of years when she and Deb turned the corners of their lives, swerved away. And if Ginger was doing the driving, well, she was always doing the driving.

I liked hugging the shoulder, but college had put me in the passing lane, and my car didn't have a fifth gear. If all I have are sports and car comparisons, that just means I'm a guy from Detroit. I can fix a lot of things, but not my own life, and if that's a little trite, I can find another sports or cars metaphor for you.

•••

Deb and I missed Roe versus Wade by a year. The two most vivid memories of my life: Ginger taking us to the clinic in Canada, and Ginger spreading her legs on the La-Z-Boy.

The long night in Windsor, right across the Detroit River, was our biggest secret—cluster of secrets, really. Corpse-flower bloom of secrets. Ginger came with us as Deb's alibi: the twins going to Niagara Falls on a road trip. Ginger planned it, having taken a similar trip herself a year earlier. Abortions were not openly contemplated in our Catholic neighborhood. You had your baby, and either you gave it away and came back to school to gut it out, or you kept it, dropped out, got married, and gutted that out instead.

•••

"If we're going to hell, we're going to hell together," Ginger said. We drove over the Ambassador Bridge to Windsor, but we came back through the Detroit–Windsor Tunnel, not glorious enough to have a fancy name. The road to hell, scenic or not, required tolls in both directions.

We'd heard the story of a teenager sticking his head out a car window and getting decapitated in the tunnel. I kept my head inside. Ginger drove. Debbie's head lay on my lap—sick with what we'd done.

Things hadn't worked out—blood, and a mad panicked blur.

I'd stood outside with Ginger and waited, trembling with fear and rage in the cold rain of early April. The doctor told us Deb could never have a baby now. We smoked Canadian cigarettes—called Next—bought from a machine in the lobby.

Ginger had taken care of hers all by herself—that was Ginger. She grabbed my hand and held it. "It wasn't like this," she said. "I swear." We whispered prayers together—an Our Father, a Hail Mary—like penance after confession.

It could have happened sooner given our carelessness—half rhythm method, half pulling out early. Ken had given me some rubbers. I'd used them up, then never bought any myself. I guess maybe we imagined we'd be together forever anyway.

We stood half in the rain under the narrow overhang of the modest clinic on a dull side street—how did Ginger ever do it alone? She called home with a tale of a flat tire and how everything was closed for some Canadian holiday. My parents thought I was camping with friends. Next—what kind of name is that for a cigarette?

How could I abandon her after that, heading off to college while she worked as a receptionist for the cavity-crazed dentist next to Helene's Beauty Shop, dying inside, thinking about that baby and how she could never have another?

•••

"You still in the house on Wilde?" Ginger asked.

"It's haunted, but it's paid for," I replied.

"I'll send you a Christmas card next year," she said.

I almost said, how about a Valentine instead, mad with her proximity, the revival of my own dead twin, the one with desire.

"I don't get many cards," I said.

"You have to send me one back," she said. "That's how it works."

"I don't know where you live," I said. "Do you live with Deb?" I asked.

"Sometimes," she said, then she went silent, sipping her beer. I noticed lipstick rimming her glass.

"Remember that snow, dude?" Sam said, poking me. He seemed at a loss in the presence of Ginger. If he was calling the signals, nobody was listening.

•••

I don't know what will happen next Christmas. The carols never change, but we only have to listen to them a couple of weeks a year, so when we blow the dust off, they seem fresh again, however briefly. On the other hand, our lives on repeat? That can make anyone crazy.

I hate stories that end in bars or football games. Someone gets drunk and does something stupid. Someone wins, someone loses. We get up the next day and move on. Those playing fields seem skewed, senses altered by alcohol or adrenaline. But sometimes the smell of fresh popcorn lingers.

...

I had no adrenaline flowing that night I spent on the bench, knee coated in green slime that burned beneath my kneepad but cured nothing. I turned away to watch pure joy rise from the cinders—two sets of twins spiraling and flipping, defying gravity—despite Eight Mile being both a school and a road that doubled down on gravity, gravity pushing against us until we cried uncle and tossed our ambition in the trash with our diplomas and took our place on the assembly line. That game clearly had no consequences. The consequences came later, long after the scoreboard ticked down to zero, long after the night janitor flipped the big switch and the field went dark. Even cheerleaders can't defy gravity forever.

...

I don't know how many bars in America are named the Alibi, but I know of at least a few and I'm not exactly a world traveler. Oh, I've been around the block a few times—the same block over and over. The assumption must be that we all need an alibi. There's only one thing I've ever needed an alibi for. I was always where I said I'd be, and no one ever seemed to doubt it. Debbie could have used that in her defense at our divorce proceedings, had she needed any defense. "I got nothing," is what I said, opening my hands to reveal that nothing. How can you argue with potato chips in your underwear?

Maybe I should have given my unused alibis to Ginger—I suspect she's needed a few over the years. But maybe she's always been the kind of person who has no need for alibis. Maybe she could give them to Debbie. To Deb. Does it matter what I call her?

•••

Christmas flu, despite being divorced for over five years.

"We should've had that kid," I said to Ginger. Maybe we'd gone through with the abortion because that's what Ginger had done. But if Deb had the baby, it might've been because that's what our parents had done. The girls we knew who'd had babies and returned to school seemed miserable.

"I would've married her," I said.

"You did marry her."

"That was different," I said, in over my head, as always. "What happened to Gino?"

She gave an enormous shrug. "I've been married twice since then," she said.

"Look at us, Bear," Sam said. "Ginger with three exes, and me with two. You and Deb lasted longer than any of our marriages. You guys got twenty good years together." He was rounding up, but I didn't say anything.

"Twenty good years," Ginger echoed, raising her glass. "You've got us beat!"

The whole table began to chant, "Twenty good years, twenty good years," pounding their glasses against the table.

The sweat was either sizzling down my back or turning cold, but I could feel it. Though the chant quickly died down, the old cheerleaders had belted it out loud enough to turn heads.

Ginger put her hand on top of mine and squeezed.

Sam leaned over from the other side. "So, fuck you, Bear," he said. "You and your twenty good years."

I didn't know what to say. "Fuck you, too," I said.

•••

"Remember that time in the living room when you spread your legs?" I bent over into Ginger's open arms as she made her way out of the Alibi. "Ginger, sometimes I wanted you so bad," I blurted suddenly.

You idiot, I can hear Ken say when I tell him, and I will.

"Which time?" she said, laughing. "I was always spreading my legs for you. Maybe you only noticed once." She stretched her arms to try to reach her hug around me. I felt her small, delicate hands gently patting my thick shoulders through my jacket.

"I was a little jealous sometimes. Or bored," she whispered. "You know me . . ." She laughed again, almost sadly. "Or, at least you knew me then."

"I wouldn't have slept with you though," she added, with a genuine smile. I smiled back. She might've emphasized *slept* or *you*. It didn't matter.

I knew it was true, and she knew I knew. We both loved her sister. I'd meant to say something about Debbie, to open that door a crack and let me breathe the complex comfort of that old familiar air. What was I thinking? *That* didn't make any sense.

"Tell Debbie how great I look," I shouted, and everyone laughed. It never felt so good to be full of shit, knowing I didn't need or want saving.

"Oh, Chris," she said loudly, "We'll always have Niagara Falls." She was laughing. Laughing and trembling. I didn't blush. She finally pulled away. I'd been further north than any of the rest of them, even Sam.

"Niagara Falls? What the hell?" Sam asked as she headed toward the door—admiring every swaying step, I imagine.

I felt as if I'd been brought back to life by a swarm of cheerleaders. I'd always had some decent moves for a big guy, and I did a little sway of my own, spilling popcorn like spare change. Popcorn taking its revenge on potato chips. Popcorn piling up like light snow.

If it makes any sense, I'm looking for that thing between floating and crashing. I guess most people just call it life. But if you're looking, you might be surprised by light streaming in the open door behind someone walking away. You thought it was already dark out there.

"Boomer," I said. "Did you ever smoke a Next cigarette?"

Attack of the Killer Antz, the Rice Method of Recovery, and Other Fables from the Crypt

Remarkably, DreamWorks' Antz *and Pixar's* A Bug's Life *were released within six weeks of each other. . . . Both films have worker ants as heroes, saving their colony and falling for a princess in the process.*

Ants swarmed over our porch ceiling like discordant musical notes released from their scales. They raced down wooden pillars and over the cracked concrete floor. Out of nowhere and suddenly. One ant played the fife, another limped, and another played drums. Somewhere, a queen had given the signal.

Or maybe that was in a movie about ants I saw with my kids when they were young. Two ant movies—*Antz* and *A Bug's Life*, animated by rival studios—came out at the same time, confusing everyone. Which fast food joint was giving away toys from which movie? They seemed to have the same plot: a misfit ant who finds God. We saw them both, but I wasn't paying much attention, half asleep in a dark theater of manic children. I would fail the *Bug's Life* vs. *Antz* showdown trivia quiz. My kids, Sid and Anna, might do better, but it's not something we compare notes on in our random and infrequent phone calls. *Antz*. That *z* jazzed up such a pedestrian word. I started uzing *z*'s instead of *s*'s because I myself needed jazzing up. My marriage was sagging. Maybe I was dragging it down, slumped into a nostalgic torpor for all my abandoned bad habits. In a way, I'd cleaned up my life. In another way, everything I'd sucked up sat inside me like a vacuum cleaner bag overflowing with dust, but I had no new bag to replace it with.

The kids are mostly grown and living time zones away from Detroit, where I take comfort in the stark clarity—cement, brick, straight, flat roads, proximity to Canada. They're off with their mother, sending back beautiful pictures of their beautiful lives that will not fade, unlike the cheap color photos we took when they were children. Color faded to an indistinct pinkish hue in the old albums—the ones with dried-up Stickum that failed to hold the photos in place any longer. When, in my nostalgic moments for tiny ants that only showed up for crumbs and sweet stuff, I pull out one of the albums shelved next to the dusty cookbooks, all the photos slide out of the pages like those ants boogie-woogying down the pillars—like "Surf's up, dude!" The neat lies of those ordered albums tumble into chaos on the floor.

•••

The real ants—big black carpenter ants—are quietly invading in their bumbling yet direct script across the gutters, soffit, fascia, down the pillars, and over the cracked cement I'm standing on.

I've always enjoyed killing ants. Even outdoors, which can fairly be considered their turf. I used to sit on my parents' porch on hot summer days smushing ants with a popsicle stick after I'd finished slurping down the colored, frozen sugar water. A couple of sweet red drops melt to the cement, then word gets out, then squish. Squish. Like the grim pleasure of pouring hydrogen peroxide on infected cuts to watch it foam up, or popping pimples as a teenager, despite all warnings against it. One of my kids, Sid, was (or is?) a cutter, which horrified me and my second wife, Del, the kids' mother. We purged the house of every sharp thing, though we missed a tiny red pencil sharpener, the size of a large grape. And we missed the great outdoors, and every sharp thing that cut him out there. And every sharp word in our failed marriage.

Last I heard, my first wife, Clare, had gone to Bazookia as a missionary for a year. Too busy keeping track of Del and the kids and negotiating through the losses. Del and I agreed on one thing: our divorce was my fault. She used to tell me that, if I had an affair, she'd cut my balls off. At least she didn't do that. The kids were at the opposite of good ages for handling it: thirteen and fourteen. They knew exactly what I did. I must have had a death wish about marriage. That was the squeaky hinge of my life—the end of that marriage.

Okay, listen, Anna and Sid. I'm just trying to explain why I lost track of Clare. I'm not blaming your mother.

•••

Why did I take such pleasure then? Why do I take such pleasure now? That small cruelty you can get away with—the lack of blood, the miniscule and brief evidence of their existence. The easy justification—the little ants eat our food, and the big ones eat our houses. The traps. The poison.

The poison that kills them, the poison we feed on. There's a whole series of horror movies about giant ants due to guys like me. Ants getting revenge. We are ants, too, though. Somebody's ants. And if you believe in God, we are God's ants, and God holds the popsicle stick. And sometimes it drips down some sweetness, and we briefly imagine a place called heaven.

I've never been a fan of heaven. Even today, when we're burying Clare, I can't imagine her there. She'd be miserable. I've always hated when people say what the dead would have liked or not liked, but Clare, in heaven? Traditional heaven? With no vices to lean on, she'd lose her balance and fall all the way through purgatory and down to hell, where I can imagine her smiling, conspiring to drive Satan crazy.

Clare had a death wish, like a carnival ride that goes amok. Enjoyable at first, adrenaline pumping, *wow, this is fun, I feel so alive*, then it goes off the tracks into space and you're asking, *is it supposed to do this*? Like the cartoons where the coyote runs off the cliff into air and doesn't fall until he looks down.

The moral of that story is supposed to be "don't look down," but I believe you have no choice. What's heaven if you can't look down on someone or something?

Clare looked down and saw something she didn't like.

Eternal life vs. heaven, twelve rounds, championship bout, cage match.

•••

Big. Black. Ants. Carpenter ants eating trails through our soft wet wood due to roof neglect. Us, me and my current partner Robin. Del (Delphinia) was my first real wife, I used to tell people, but I'm not going to throw Clare under the bus now. She threw herself under the bus.

I pause after that mean thing. Meaner than you think. Suicide. Meaner than that, given various chances to intervene. Del was my excuse to avoid Clare, during and after that marriage. Clare was like a kid, and I couldn't afford another kid. I had my own problems. I had a cutter loose in the house.

Some churches say you'll go to hell if you commit suicide. They probably say that because otherwise we'd all be killing ourselves to get to heaven sooner, right?

•••

One early evening in late April, years ago, I was alone on a trail in the park across the street—a trail I still walk on after work—working the same job I worked then—"Mr. Handyman," where I am one of many, not the Mr. Handyman, who signs my checks Joey Stewart. When I came over the slight rise up from Panther Hollow, I ran into Sid walking toward me with another boy—both maybe thirteen. Looking at them together, I suddenly saw everything clearly: they were looking to have sex in the rising greenery of spring in that large, urban park full of hiding places. Who would've thought they'd run into old Dad taking his constitutional? "Hi," I said, and kept walking, and neither of us said a word to each other or anyone in the family about that ever, but shortly after, he started making those cuts on his arms and legs. I, the ex-junkie husband of junkie Clare, never noticed all his long sleeves of summer.

Hey, I used to shoot heroin. At least you're not doing that. Never do that. Hey, we have something in common, isn't that cool? I used to shoot up between my toes, can you believe it, ha ha ha. Don't do that. Stop cutting. Start talking to me. Your mother saved me, but that didn't save our marriage.

Here's what I did tell him: *We'll find someone for you to talk to.* I was a handyman by default. Something I picked up on the fly, once I stopped stealing from my own family. Once I dropped Clare off at rehab and drove away forever. Who said talk is cheap?

I was used to sweeping up, leaving no evidence. It's never that simple. For example, I did not drive away forever. Forever, only in my imagination. In my revised version where ants aren't raining down on me.

•••

I was on a first-name basis with the exterminator, Metallica, due to previous encounters with the entire range of invasive urban pests. I even had a customer loyalty card, a three-by-five blank notecard that he'd punch a hole in every time he came out.

After I sprayed the porch with my over-the-counter stuff, the reinforcement ants emerged from wherever their nest was, and I gave up and made the call. Metallica clearly does not give a shit about self-poisoning. He wears no protective gear, lugging around his tank of poison, flashing his gap-toothed grin. I know a lot of people like that, given my personal history. But bug killer doesn't even get you high.

"Dude," he said, clanking up the steps, the tank bouncing off his leg. He shook my hand forcefully, perhaps to remind me that we're in this together. Remember to wash that hand, I tell myself.

"Might want to fix that roof," he says, peering up at wet, rotting boards. "Aren't you the handyman?"

"I am just one of his minions," I said.

"You're one deep motherfucking bullshitter," he said, spitting his poison saliva over the porch railing.

After he sprayed into the holes he'd drilled, ants came raining down. That's not just an expression. A literal storm of ants, falling to their deaths, having all looked down.

"Impressive," I said from behind the screen door.

"You're gonna need an ant umbrella to come out here," he said.

I didn't let him into the house. I handed off the check in the doorway.

He smoked as he worked. He had a precision trigger finger on the hose, but his smoking fingers always trembled.

"It's not my fault they came back," he said as he punched my note card.

...

I never told Robin much about Clare. I told her Del was my first legal wife. Clare, Del, then Robin. Don't mix them up like I have.

When Robin found me crying in the bathtub, she had a few questions:

"I thought she wasn't a real wife?" Not exactly a question, but a comment that demanded response. I didn't cry much, but when I did, the bathtub was my go-to spot.

"She had an in with God and got us annulled," I said.

"I thought you just lived together. What other secrets you got for me, bathing beauty," she said. That wasn't a question either.

I tore some toilet paper off the roll and blew my nose.

"I was high most of the time, so I'm sure I forgot a few things. You've never seen me high. Consider yourself lucky."

"Lucky is not the word for what I'm feeling," she said. "I'm not jealous about Del. It's like we're even—with me and Teddy Boy. But now, you're one up on me."

"Not according—" I was going to make a joke about the Pope but started crying again. I was holding something in and cutting myself or injecting myself wasn't going to let it out. Because it was in me—a version of myself I had to own up to and mourn at the same time.

•••

I once got up in the middle of the night to pee and found two-year-old Anna sitting in the empty bathtub in the dark.

"Oh, hi, Dad," she said, like I was dropping in on her to borrow a cup of bubbles. She seemed so at home, sitting in a bathtub in silent darkness. If only life could be that simple again, Safe. She knew she was safe there.

•••

"Oh, hi, Robin," I said, once I stopped that shivering shoulder thing I get when I'm on a crying jag. Which only ever happens when Hailey's Comet passes by.

•••

"We got married on a dare and enough speed to keep us awake till we got to Vegas."

"And that lasted exactly how long?"

Robin had survived her own bad marriage and had no interest in tying the knot again. I think she was asking more out of curiosity. She made a good living as a family court judge and didn't want me suing for support, since my odd jobs resulted in an odd level of income much lower than hers.

"We lived together for a year or so before, but marriage was the kiss of death and we—well, actually, she—got it annulled. They didn't have computers back then, but you can see the remnants of our marriage on some erasable typing paper up in the attic with the bishop's signature and seal."

"In the eyes of God," she said. "You weren't married *in the eyes of God*." Robin repeated with an eye roll. She inherited cynicism from her father, an immigrant who had seen bodies stacked up in churches back in Croatia after World War II.

"Isn't God blind?"

"That's justice. And that's a lie too."

"Clare found God in a jail cell, and God told her to dump that loser and get straight, and so, annulment."

"In light of recent events, God wasn't enough," Robin said.

I got up out of the empty bathtub, fully clothed. "I hate that phrase, 'in light of recent events,'" I said.

She looked at me like she was going to respond, her lips briefly parted, to defend that phrase. But we had been together for three years, and she knew that the phrase wasn't what it was about.

I stormed out onto the front porch to have a little talk with the ants.

•••

Clare was thirty-three. Not the twenty-seven club, but the Jesus club. When someone dies young, suddenly it's a contest to see who can grieve the most. To possess the death. The ants carry away the dead bodies to be consumed back in their crib up in my rafters. When someone dies young, it's like somebody spiked the funeral home Kool-Aid with grief pills. The spiraling wails, the random fleeing, grieving bodies bouncing off walls like the blind, colliding into each other and comingling tears into a swamp of grief. The ant-like frenzy in response to poison, the sudden spazzing into death.

Above the ants on this humid morning, a hawk drifts effortlessly on breezes we're not feeling down here. Why don't we have a more effortless word than "effortlessly"? It stumbles out of our mouths, trips on sidewalk cracks.

•••

Clare, who I am mourning later—mourning now—was like a returning ant circling the porch after the magic poison has done its job, saying, "Hey, where'd everybody go?" The overeager kid wanting a playmate. Good luck with that, Metallica would say.

•••

No, when she killed herself, she was saying, "No more playmates for me. I'm blowing this pop(sicle) stand." You can buy that on a mug now. They should put a warning on it: Do not drink poison from this cup.

•••

We are all cannibals, of course.

•••

Hey, ant, come over here so I can squish you, and you can join your friends!

I sweep the dead off the porch, and they land on the driveway, little crunchy commas splicing apart complete sentences.

•••

The ant carries around the poison powder on its little feet, then slows down. Then stops to think about the meaning of life. Then learns the meaning of life.

•••

If all the ants die, who will be left to eat them? I admire them for dragging their dead off the battlefield, even if it is to be their dinner. Get rid of the bodies. Get on with it.

Clare wasn't young and wasn't old. She fell and keeps on falling, her mad whisper keeping that hawk aloft.

•••

RICE: Rest, Ice, Compression, Elevation.

I sprained my ankle last week, tripping over a pipe in the bathroom I was working on. A job I still need to finish, according to a phone message from Mr. Handyman. I'm wearing one of those stupid black medical boots that make you limp.

I'll be clomping around in it at the funeral. They call them celebrations of life these days, but she wasn't exactly celebrating life when she took those pills. It's what her parents are calling it. They, who wanted to know if we lit the Unity Candle at our wedding. We came back from Vegas wearing cheap rings, and that's what they wanted to know. Elvis didn't have one, I said. Didn't they know we were a couple of pyromaniacs? They knew me from when I was a popsicle boy.

Will they ask me about the ankle? Will they want me to say a few words? Will they speak to me at all, the survivor of sadness, the duke of denial, the king of cocaine, the asshole of AA?

Her next guy—she never married again—called me up when they split to tell me he was going to piss on my grave. Apropos of nothing except having heard some version of our life together. Who was he to say?

"She can piss on my grave," I told him, "but you can't. I'd prefer dancing on graves rather than pissing," I said, "though I realize that from my grave I will have no say in this."

"Annulled, my ass," he said and hung up.

The last thing she said to me was, "Shut up and get a tattoo." Advice I have tried to take. Tattoo, check. Shutting up, no check. Tattoo of a series of concentric circles on my forearm. A target I once hit without fail. Bullseye!

...

Recovery is not some kind of neat acronym that follows a precise order. Ditto with the stages of grief. They can't even agree on how many stages there are—five? Seven? As if there is ever a final stage: dabda? spadtra? With all those vowels, they should have been able to come up with something. yabba dabba doo!

I'm starting with I:

ICE

The last time we spoke was at a potluck housewarming for our mutual friend Sam. I brought death-machine apple pie from the supermarket. Store-bought—too sweet, like always—what was I thinking? I brought vanilla ice cream to make it even more too sweet. I have a sweet tooth. See popsicles above.

Those in recovery usually find each other at gatherings like that. It's like llamas who smell your breath—you can feel it in the hesitations and discomfort. In the stepping outside for cigarettes. In the fact that they are not holding a brown bottle, a tumbler, or a stemmed glass. The way they trail their hands through the melting ice in the cooler as if fishing for a miracle.

The way they hold those cheap plastic water bottles that crackle when you squeeze them. The frequency of crackling. The labels floating in the cooler, the cheap glue useless—how quick it occurs, the release of the label. Then, anything can happen.

•••

For a grown man, I still eat a lot of popsicles. So many flavors now! Mango! Watermelon! Coconut! Happiness! That kid on the porch was stuck with grape, orange, and cherry—and he only liked cherry. And he never got up the nerve to walk across the street to talk to the cute girl on her porch whose nervous twitch he could spot, even from that distance. Not until he started drinking and redefined sweetness into an unpopular flavor that she fled from, only to get pregnant with a football star's baby. Kid! Kid! Maybe she would have squished some ants with you! Maybe you could have shared that sugar high!

Her parents took care of the baby, as in taking her to Canada to have an abortion. She said he raped her.

He raped her.

•••

Okay, Clare was that girl on the porch. Okay, okay. Ice is good for numbing. For a time, I was addicted to cubes. I bit into them and drove Del crazy.

•••

We kept some of those plastic *Bug's Life/Antz* McHappy Burger King meal giveaways. How do you make an ant smile? Bright lime green ants. Tossed in the blue plastic barrel with the zoo animals and dinosaurs, the *Star Trek/Wars/ET*s, the antique trolls and gnomes. We might've finally thrown them away during one of the many purges, or, maybe they're in Del's base-ment—she has the sentimental gene. The savior gene. But once I was saved, then what? Dullsville, and even giant fluorescent ants couldn't perk us up once the kids were teenagers. Even if we stepped on them barefoot and fell moaning to the floor.

...

Clare brought downer salad and ballistic dressing to Sam's. We made small talk for big kids. "There's no I in Clare," she always told me and everyone else.

"When did you first hear the word "balsamic," I asked. "When we were kids, I thought balsamic was a variation on Greek Orthodox. Nobody in the old neighborhood was Greek."

She sighed. "I know I shouldn't care," she said. "Why won't you talk to me?"

"You shouldn't," I said. "If I didn't care, I'd be talking to you."

"Oh," she said, "It's the old, 'it's me, not you.'"

"I didn't say that, yet" I said. "I'm saving it for the pie."

I did not want to admit I couldn't keep up with her mania—a common path, I know now, from drug addict to religious zealot, from murderer to religious zealot. The Win and Wang of addiction and belief. She wasn't going to hold still, even for Jesus. If I died, she would've abandoned me on the side of the road, my inability to keep up seriously compromised by death. Then they'd come by and scrape me up and throw me in the back of the truck with the other dead bodies. The Antz, just on a larger scale. And maybe that was okay.

"Are you eating a lot of carrots?" I asked. "Your skin looks orange."

"It's called healthy, Harry." She rolled her eyes. "You were just used to the junkie pallor. I've moved way up on the color wheel. You, on the other hand, still look kind of invisible," she said. "No offense."

"I still feel kind of invisible," I said, pierced by one of those old love arrows, love-slivers that never quite get removed. Slivers of slivers dug in deep. "It's a different invisible. The wife-and-kids invisible."

"You're not happy? Wasn't that one wife ago?"

"Sometimes I miss killing myself. I mean, almost. Isn't there a middle ground? I could use just a tad more obliviousness."

"I wouldn't know," she said. "I'm still an extremist." She smiled mysteriously.

She was a killer bee, and in lieu of having someone to sting, she stung herself. I didn't see it coming, mistaking energy for invincibility.

•••

"It's good to see you two talking," Sam said.

"Why's that?" I asked.

"Yeah, why?" she asked.

We exchanged The Smile. Capital T Capital S.

This smile that said "I don't really want to smile, but I just can't help it." The smile I had for no one else.

REST

My leg tensed on the chair she had once sat in. The porch chair that survived her and Del and moved with me to Robin. Clare did not have a favorite chair. I was going to say that she did, but she didn't. She'd sit anywhere. She was one of those people who preferred the floor. Wrought iron—new cushions, but the same frame. Overwrought iron—the same joke I used with all of them at various points.

My ankle only hurts when I laugh, so I am not laughing. I don't want to go to the funeral. Just like I did not want to answer her calls and texts. I wasn't going to mention them—a little secret from Del and Robin—Clare had in recent weeks been buzzing my phone and sending cryptic texts like "Howdy Sailor" and not so cryptic like "Call me, you asshole, I don't bit." No e. How could she leave me without the e?

I was thinking about cutting and pasting some of her texts in here, but it turns out I deleted them all, though I saved some emails from BEFORE. The peppy, jazzy, funny ones that charmed me. Swept me off my feet like an ant swept off the porch. But then it turns out (the double turnout!) that I have some of them memorized. Random observations like "the wind is as crisp as a hairy coconut today" or "is your second toe still bigger than your first?"

•••

At first, it's just the little ants, but they get killed off, then the big ants show up. The little ones are almost a concept, an abstraction. Tiny specks you can almost ignore. They dutifully enter ant traps until you can shake them like maracas.

Did I spill something to attract the big ants? I did not. The big ants, they say, *You talkin' to me? I ain't going in that dark little trap, chump! Gimme some wet wood pronto*!

VICE

One of the two stages of life.

A metal tool with movable jaws that are used to hold an object firmly in place while work is done on it, typically attached to a workbench.

•••

She wanted to be swept off the porch, not buried in a box, but I had no official role as the annullee. I was just an attendee.

I'm glad I didn't join her in ant-arctica. But the loss of her electric madness was shorting me out with grief. Two children on identical shy slabs of cement ran away from the ants only to swallow the poison themselves. How do you warm a house? Not with explosives. Not with spilled blood from precise cuts.

Del called to inform me of Clare's death. She thought I'd want to know. Tomorrow I will join the ants on the freeway to the funeral. She'd been living on an organic farm outside the city where the workers covered up their tattoos for their fancy farm-to-table dinners. Some kind of cult, though we're all in some cult, even if it's a cult of one. How long will the receiving line be? Not very, I'm guessing. Unless it's at the methadone clinic.

•••

When my father died, he'd outlived all his friends except Lenny, a former ice cream novelties salesman from our old neighborhood in Detroit.

"I'm the last one," Lenny said. With a note of triumph, or resignation? I wanted to ask, but lunch was being served in the retirement home in Florida where his kids had stashed him. He complained about the paper cups of ice cream they served. "Not ice cream at all," he said. "Some fake over-frozen vanilla stuff with the cheap wooden spoon that can't put a dent in it. They think we'll hurt ourselves if we had real spoons. Whoever hurt themself with a spoon?" Lenny was a Bomb Pop afficionado who did not believe in the simple, the colorless, the bland. In truth, my father did not like talking on the phone to Lenny in Florida. My father was not a talker like the ice cream salesman.

"He could sell ice cream to Eskimos," my father said.

"You can't call them Eskimos anymore," I said.

My father made my children shake hands with him. No hugging or kissing. No "I love you's." This isn't an excuse. He believed in a firm grip, and it got him through. We all have to figure that out on our own, not just do what our parents do.

"Lenny, the Bomb Pop had a fatal flaw," I told him. "You couldn't get the whole damn thing in your mouth, so it dripped all over your hand."

"Ralph," he called me, which was my father's name. "You got a small mouth. You're full of shit, like always."

•••

Then the flies start showing up, then the wasps. I have never seen a movie about cute flies on a dung pile, or wasps in their paper nests, but bees get a pass, due to honey.

What's an occasional sting if it means honey in the long run? A conundrum of addiction.

Maybe I should stop being such a smartass. That's the kind of logic that can turn you into a junkie. Clare, nodding off, sprawled in a slumped insubstantial pose. Human lumps of clay, we were unwilling to be molded into purpose except to obtain more.

•••

Wasp spray shoots up to twenty feet. Or the distance from heaven to earth. The wasps crawl out of their nests like junkies during a bust, then tumble to earth to twitch briefly and die. Maybe I don't have to tell you, but I enjoy blasting it across the driveway into the eaves of the garage, safe in the killing.

•••

Life is an ant trap. Safe in the killing.

•••

ICE

Nobody move.
Crinkly water bottles swimming in it.

•••

ORTHO. RAID. ROUNDUP. HOME DEFENSE. REAL KILL. DIAZINON. DEET. CUTTER. COMBAT MAX *with Accushot sprayer.* CAPTAIN JACK'S DEADBUG BREW. HOT SHOT *with Egg Kill!* BUG STO(M)P.

•••

Her parents sent out bounty hunters to find a minister to do the service. Where's Elvis when you need him?

•••

Del, though sympathetic on the phone, wasn't coming all the way up from Houston. She was living with Tom, a friend of ours from way back. Tom helped her move out of the house then took her down to Houston to start over. With my kids. What a pal, Tom. They used to bowl in a league with Clare. In Detroit, everybody bowls. Church groups, methadone clinicians, ice cream salesmen.

Life is full of fallback positions, but we need to get through the first thirty years or so before we have enough of them lined up behind us. Like that fun game where you fall backward and trust someone to catch you. You need a bunch of people back there to increase the odds of somebody stepping up. Some are just going to let you fall. Who let Clare fall, finally? Or, who did Clare feel she could finally trust to let herself fall? She was sending out her SOS texts, and I was killing ants on the porch, afraid to step across the street yet again.

Yes, I let her fall—I'm on the list. I thought she was just going to tie her shoe then get back up. I blame it on the naivety pills the doctor put me on. I blame it on me, but that's our little secret. I have an emergency appointment scheduled after the funeral with the pill doctor.

I need to go in order to prove to myself that I did not abandon her. That she abandoned me, then circled back, thinking I'd still be there. But then I had kids to take to ant movies and then superhero movies and then teen rom-com movies. Somebody has to buy the popcorn, which reminds me:

RICE

Ice it. Ice it or heat it, the eternal debate. Obviously, I made the wrong choice.

The science behind RICE has never been tested. Everybody just likes the mnemonic device. Hell, it took me forever just to learn how to spell *mnemonic*. Just how many words have an *m* and *n* together at the beginning like that?

If ants had dog tags, this battlefield would sparkle with their deaths. Tiny pieces of Safe-T-Glass around their necks.

ICE

The brief pleasure of numbness to calm the tissue. To begin healing.

COMPRESSION

Clare and I compressed ourselves together and for a brief time healed each other or distracted each other or sweat and slid against each other as if we could live forever without *effort*. Without *lessly*.

Lost in the weeds. I like getting lost in the weeds, hidden in greenery. By greenery. Surrounded by it, off the main road, the wild, uncultivated sprawl. The drugs were hidden there. Lotz of bugz in those weeds.

I'd put myself in the vice in the first place. Vice—all those definitions squeezed together.

•••

BUG'Z LIFE VS. ANTZ

I wanted to carry that *z* with me everywhere, the simple joy of the kids holding my hands in the dark, but that was just another illusion/mirage/shadow puppet of God.

I know I am repeating myself. At least I'm not in the bathtub anymore. Am I at the funeral yet? Did anyone eat my store-bought pie?

The funeral—no, I'm skipping it. It never happened or didn't happen yet or is happening as I speak. She didn't want one. Her parents were extremely helpful with the annulment, if you know what I mean, so I wasn't looking forward to seeing them see me, that page in their dead girl's life that tore when they tried to erase it.

What am I saying? They're not going to care about me paying my respects. They'd taken my respects a long, long time ago. To hell with respects, I'd be thinking if I was them. That same thought was hollowing out my chest, even if I was partly grieving for myself. Maybe that's what Robin knew in that bathroom. I wasn't heaving my chest like that and stuttering grief for lost love. And not to show off, exaggerate the grief like in that funeral home whose floor was electrified with it. No, it was for me.

•••

Ashes to ashes, dust to dust. In a borrowed urn, they sit. It looks like Jesus was still hanging around until the end. I don't know what kind of story she told him before she said her goodbyes.

•••

Flies crawl and ants fly. How did we end up here?

Once, when Del and I were still married, we flew to France to renew our vows.

Don't ever renew your vows. It's almost as stupid as throwing a baggy full of speed in the car and driving to Vegas to get married.

Del and I did not get married by an Elvis impersonator.

Once, a swarm of bees took up residence between the shutter and window in our garage. We called a beekeeper, who was glad to take them away to make honey and money for him. One person's pest is another person's . . . pest. Who can I call to take away the ant colony?

I keep thinking we should have found a way to live with the bees, who had no interest in us. *I* should have found a way.

•••

Clare made a death playlist, and it was not the sound of bees buzzing. I might put bees on mine if I leave the world behind on my own terms like she did. I can't say I won't. But I want to say it.

I don't know what's on her playlist. Sam heard about it from her parents. They trust Sam.

•••

Music has its limitations, though I have been a fan of Wishful Thinking. I have all their albums. I like the warped vinyl of my youth the best. I like when it skips, when it goes back, then forward again.

Sam and his current partner Jan made Coma Playlists, imagining what songs might bring them out of one. They are co-presidents of the Wishful Thinking fan club. Jan admits to sleeping with their lead singer back in her wild days.

•••

In France, the designated driver is named Sam. Del and I had some good meals there before we came home and got divorced. Sam I Am until the end of my days.

•••

Ants tremble in their death throes. Are there any other kind of throes?

Once, I could catch flies in my hands. A wasp stung me when I opened the empty mail box when we got home from France. When you leave, there's always someone else moving in. Nature abhors a vacuum, Aristotle supposedly said, and that was before the invention of vacuum cleaners. Before the abandonment of the word *abhors.*

•••

I miss the bee hive. The sweet dripping buzz.

Ant traps, roach motels, mosquito condos, pigeon high-rises of death. Human fireball death traps. Oh, to go out like a human fireball. Without the pain, I mean. Is life a bee hive or ant trap? Do we "check in but never check out" like the commercials say?

I took one wrought-iron chair. The chairs come in pairs, but Clare was traveling light. She took a poster of a cat saying *Hang in There.*

Don't make a mountain out of a molehill or a pile of beans out of an anthill. Everything stings.

Love doesn't matter so much anymore. Sadly, I've settled. No more crazy *z*'s for me.

•••

Since I have nothing to ignore now that Clare has died, I worry about falling flat on my face. I'll never lean back and wait to be caught. I should stop killing ants. The ants should be smart enough to ignore me. The great outdoors awaits them. All theirs. I concede. The bathtub awaits.

•••

Now, they say swelling is good. The hawk disappeared into the trees. The extreme heat is killing pine trees. A bored borer is killing palm trees. Some drunken bug is killing grape vines. It's still mostly green out there, and I'll take mostly green.

•••

I twisted my ankle dancing on the head of a pin.

•••

Which brings us to ELEVATE
    RICE. Or do I have it mixed up, and it's really ERIC?
    An empty porch chair overly wrought on the porch, surrounded by dead ants curled into specks of mourning. I am the one twitching.

•••

ELEVATE
    Keep it higher than your heart, they say.

Serpentine Drive

R ain had been predicted, and the lumbering mass of dark clouds rolling slowly across the sky promised it. Seven thirty. Early enough to miss the crowds flocking to Belle Isle for the daily recess from quarantine. The lions at either end of the bridge wore face masks.

In these times of fear and panic, Jonah often projected himself forward like a felled tree. His height, six feet, the recommended distance between humans. If he hit no one on his way down, he was safe to die by his own method. Lisa, his live-in partner, was the only member of his quarantine group, since his parents had kicked them out of theirs due to safety concerns. You could be careless in your fears and your lack of fears. You could fall down like a tree and see if you might take someone down with you.

Lisa, a sometime actor, sometime stand-up comedian, had a current income of absolute zero. Jonah, a laid-off dealer at the Ambassador Casino, had filed for unemployment. He hoped it'd be coming in soon, along with the government bribe check that everyone was getting. Spring hope was suffocating under piles of discarded face masks and latex gloves.

She kept trying to hold his hand as they walked up the empty road that twisted through the park past the abandoned par-three golf course. It had been named after a deceased mayor who'd hung out in the dilapidated clubhouse and played cards with other local pols during the day, and at night played blackjack at the Ambassador. Jonah and Lisa did not golf or gamble.

"What's with the handholding?" Jonah asked, knowing he should just keep his mouth shut. She'd told him yesterday she wanted to leave him when the deadly dust settled.

•••

"The virus is a sign," she'd said. At the kitchen table, she was peeling a grapefruit. The smell tweaked the stale air in their grungy apartment, reminding him of the other big disaster they'd survived back in Key West where they met—Hurricane Wilma. It took down all the grapefruit from the one tree in front of their building, and since they'd returned promptly from evacuation, they reaped the benefits. They filled basketfuls to haul back to their sweaty apartment without power. They squeezed them for juice, eating them with their hands in the dark, the white pulp wedging itself under their nails. The refreshing tang lingered on their hands and faces as they made love for lack of something better to do in the silent darkness and sweat.

•••

For lack of something better to do, she held his hand.

"Don't be mean," she said. "We had a good run." Though she let go. A lone car twisted down Serpentine Drive toward them, and he slipped behind her into single file on the side of the road.

"I thought we were still running," Jonah said. He'd have to clap his muddy shoes together before they went back inside.

"Glad I got a haircut before all this," he said, running his hand through stiff, unwashed hair.

"Remember when you tried dyeing it." she said. "I'm sorry."

"What?" he said, though he'd heard.

"I'm sorry I asked you to dye it. What did I think it mattered?"

...

The silence of no cars returned, and the thick clouds seemed to cushion it. Late March, the trees just beginning to bud, their wet, black bones still visible, returning birds who knew no lockdown whistling through those bones.

A flock of dull brown birds suddenly started pecking holes in the clouds, their screeching amplified by the twisting road. Like they were going mad with power, not used to having the stage to themselves. They were either mating or killing each other. Three blue jays duked it out, then dispersed to three separate trees as if a bell had rung between rounds.

Squirrels looked aggrieved as they dug random holes and ran frantic up and down trees and across the park's green edge of lawn. Some of them had nuts stuffed between their teeth like gags.

"Lighten up, squirrels," Lisa said, though Jonah knew she was talking to him.

...

They stopped at what they simply called the Ugly Monument. Neither of them touched the surface of the plain, square stone still smudged with factory grit. The plaque said it commemorated the planting of a grove of trees to honor the World War I dead. Those trees were dead too. Jonah called it the death zone and always hurried past, but today, they carefully read the tarnished plaque.

"One 'Great War,'" Lisa said. "What a concept."

"Is this 'The Great Plague'?"

"They already had The Great Plague—a bunch of them."

Suddenly, five deer exploded through the trees, nearly mowing them down. The dog who'd chased them stood proudly on the curb and watched them fade into the brush on the other side of the street.

"Fuck you," Jonah said. "Where's your owner? Where's your leash?"

"The dog doesn't control whether it's on a leash or not."

"Well, fuck the owner in absentia." Jonah looked up the hill behind the dog but saw only the black bones. Bones, and some yellow sprays of forsythia.

"For someone who does stand-up, you do a lot of sitting down," he said.

"What?"

"That's the joke I told you when we met. I'm getting nostalgic."

"You'll have more money. I'll be the one taking a chance," she said.

He wanted to ask where she would go. Because of the virus, it had seemed all too quiet, theoretical, a vague future breakup, and he'd liked it that way.

Together three years, heading out of their twenties to a less casual life with more counting and uncertainty. Most stand-up comics get a real job at age twenty-eight, he'd read online last night after she broke the news.

He'd also read that some dealers averaged fifty bucks an hour. Not in Detroit. He was making more like fifteen. His salary was around fifteen grand. How many years could he live on that?

Maybe he'd gotten too careful. At work, he was always being watched.

•••

Being locked up together lost its novelty fast. They never even finished one jigsaw puzzle. It lay in a muddle on their crooked card table propped up by unread books. Pieces had been sticking to his sweaty elbows and dropping to the floor, so Jonah wasn't even sure they had them all anymore. Flowers in a vase. It was all they could find online. No one had predicted a run on puzzles. Grocery stores, yes.

•••

An enormous empty nest, high in one of the highest trees, caught his eye and held it. Almost the size of a barrel of hay, as if dropped from the sky and caught there.

"Hawk, hawk, hawk," he said.

"Are you calling hawks now?"

He didn't answer. On the curve of the road they were headed toward, a young shaggy man-boy was looking at his phone and nodding his head like a bird to water, drinking in sounds in his headphones—music or a voice he emphatically agreed with. Jonah wanted to get close enough to him to fall down and measure distance. He was wishing he had something to nod to as emphatically as that boy. Some truth, some music. Not this breakup shit.

"At least I'm not a mime," Lisa said.

It was the first joke she'd told him. "Getting into the nostalgic spirit of this breakup, I see," he said.

"We've turned into the walking dead. You'd be arguing more, fighting more to make this work if . . . ." She stopped.

He was swallowing what she said. Even through their masks, she sounded incredibly loud on the empty road, like she was broadcasting their secret to the world. He was embarrassed that she was right, embarrassed for not fighting harder.

...

"It's good you brought the golf umbrella," she said, and they laughed. The wind-pushed rain was slanting beneath the bright red-and-white umbrella.

"I've never been golfing in my life," he said.

"I know," she said.

"I guess I've told you everything," he said. "Maybe you're right."

"I've told you everything too," she said.

"Have you, really?" he asked. "I was wondering if there's someone else."

"There sure as hell isn't," she said. "We're on fucking lockdown, you asshole."

"Right now," he said. "That's a state of mind."

"'Right now' is a state of insanity," she said.

"Why are we going this way?" he asked. She had headed down off the road onto a muddy path next to a narrow canal overflowing its banks due to the rain. She was jumping from log to log, suddenly nimble, and did not answer.

He thought about standing there forever or at least until she disappeared.

•••

The sun peeked through suddenly, against all odds. "Where's the rainbow?" he said.

"Postponed. Canceled. Quarantined. Eliminated."

"I guess rainbows were just something we hallucinated," he said. "Now that we don't believe, they've disappeared."

"Like unicorns."

"Like phoenixes."

"Like two-headed dogs."

"I've seen a two-headed dog," he said.

"I know," she said.

The Girl in the Tie-Dyed T-Shirt outside Spice Island

We sat in our battered blue Focus in front of Spice Island waiting to pick up some takeout. My wife Meg idling in the driver's seat. I sat beside her, idling also. After thirty-three years, it was the best we could do. At least we hadn't stalled. At least we weren't rolling backward down the hill. At least our kids were grown and no longer crammed into the tiny backseat.

In front of Pizza Romano next door, beside the rusty wrought-iron staircase up to the modest apartments above, a girl—college student maybe—stood with a guy—mid-twenties maybe. He looked almost wizened, though he had that calculated unshaven look that our son Charlie favored. Charlie even had a special razor attachment that left some scruff. He was gay and had no intention of giving us grandchildren in any form whatsoever. He lived in New York and patronized us with occasional visits. But hey, we loved him. I thought he spent too much time trying to look younger than he was. He mocked me for buying clothes at Target. All in the family. We looked forward to his visits. It was like having a referee in the house. Our daughter Leah was living with her boyfriend Mal in a remote village in Indiana where they scraped by doing organic farming, though mostly scraping, it seemed. We hadn't seen her in two years.

Outside Romano's, I was thinking the guy was maybe a boyfriend, but a new one. They had the choreography of that—a flirtatious glance, then away—laughter, a little loud, drifting in our open waiting-for-takeout windows. The girl wore a long, garish tie-dyed T-shirt, and maybe that was all. No short skirt or a pair of shorts peeking out under it. She circled around him, a combination of strutting and pouting. Was she mad, drunk, or very, very happy? He stood, nervously frozen, hands stuffed into the front pockets of his ratty, loose, lopsided jeans. She was animated, barely contained.

"What's taking so long?" Meg asked. We rarely answered each other anymore. Maybe we didn't need to, or maybe we had no answers.

They looked more like locals than college kids. Though some college kids were local in our neighborhood near Wayne. The girl wore loud makeup—thick mascara, bright lipstick. My father, who liked plain women like my mother, would have said she looked like a clown. A clown with no pants, I'd have said to him, if he were still idling, not stalled beneath his gravestone just a few miles away in Mount Elliot. The guy wore a white T-shirt under a leather jacket, despite the heat. The James Dean look, though he would've asked, *who's that*?

"Remember hot pants?" I said to Meg.

I'd just returned from my third colonoscopy, and I was starving. Spice Island was my go-to restaurant. I always got the same thing. Ginger salad and Singapore kai teow. They knew us. We knew them. Double comfort.

The hospital required that I have someone with me to drive home, so Meg had taken off work and we'd spent the whole day together. Though I was passed out for quite a bit of it. Just like in my druggie days, I thought but didn't say. Those days were speed bumps we'd clumsily made our way over—they'd jostled us apart for a time. I don't believe in water under the bridge, though Pittsburgh, where we once lived, claimed to be the Venice of the US due to the large number of bridges crossing its three rivers. Somebody once called it the Paris of Appalachia, but that never caught on. Steel City, it was and is. Somebody once called Detroit the Gateway to Canada. Nah. The Motor City, it was and is. Not the *blank* of any *blank*.

"Where's Joe?" she asked. Joe—the owner. His real name was something more Spice-Island-ish, but he wanted us to call him Joe. Friendly guy. Works hard. Not like that pizza guy next door who got busted selling heroin. Real name: Tony Romano. Romano's closed for a few months, then reopened. Under new management? Hard to tell, like it was hard to tell about that girl. Though I was trying very hard to tell.

She lifted one arm above her head to lean on the brick wall on the side of the building. The T-shirt rose slightly. I squinted, but, in the shadow, I could see nothing clearly. I would need to be on my knees in the gravel looking up like a perv to see for sure. I wasn't a perv, just a guy waiting for food. An old boring guy who just got his ass cleaned out again as a bonus for his brother dying of cancer. I was on the colonoscopy fast track—every five years, not ten. If my brother was still alive, I'd give him some shit about that—kidding around, like we always did, until the very end.

Was that girl teasing? Scruff-face didn't seem interested in looking. Maybe he was used to it, like I was used to Meg. Maybe he was terrified. To her, I was just a flabby arm hanging out a car window.

My doctor down at Mercy—a gastroenterologist—he needs a shorter specialty, I told him, like I'd told him five years ago—had been irritated. When I woke up, he said I wasn't cleaned out as much as I should have been. I did the usual prep—drinking the stuff, sitting on the toilet, not eating, blah blah blah. I'd drunk all the stuff. If he'd given me more stuff, I would have drunk it, damn it. If there's some shit hiding in there somewhere, don't blame me. "This is my third time," I said. "I know how to do the prep."

"Apparently not," he said. He sounded disappointed that he didn't find any polyps. Maybe I was still a bit groggy. Maybe he had five more of those to do before he called it a day.

"What are you looking at?" Meg asked.

I sighed. "I don't think that girl has any pants on," I said, regretting it already.

She pointed out her window. "That one?" The girl and the boy were looking up at us right that very second.

"Damn it, don't point," I said. "Where's Joe, I'm starving?"

"Tie-dye," she said. "Go figure."

She was concentrating now. Squinting at the girl. She shaded her eyes. The sun was starting to drop behind Romano's. We never got pizza from them, with their rats, roaches, and heroin. Joe valiantly tried to keep the pests out of his place. The empty lot between the two buildings was mined with rat and roach explosives, according to Joe. It seems contradictory to sell pizza and heroin. You don't get munchies from smack.

Even heroin can become chic. Even tie-dye can resurface. Heroin was never chic for me. Even when I craved it. Her shirt wasn't a homemade tie-dye job. It was a side-of-the-road Sunday gas station tie-dye next to the velvet paintings. Too neat, too bright. It looked pseudo tie-dye. Like stone-washed jeans. How long did those last? Now, it's ripped jeans. You pay for the strategic rips. She wore no jeans, ripped or not. Her T-shirt was strategically placed.

The girl pointed at us and laughed. Her nose wrinkled up. The guy gave us a dismissive wave of the hand.

"She thinks we're funny," I said.

"Yeah, I know," Meg said, startling me. "Bitch with no pants on."

I turned off the engine to see if I could hear them better. I'd told Meg to tell me if she ever thought I needed a hearing aid, and then last month she told me, and I said, I don't think so. But I've been secretly testing myself ever since.

"I think she's wearing short-shorts," Meg said. "Why would she be out on the street in her undies—or less—except to torture old men like you?" In the car leaving the hospital parking garage, we'd made our jokes about getting cleaned out. Those were behind us.

I wanted to say *fuck you* to both of those beautiful youngsters, but why go down that potholed road. It was my empty stomach wanting to say that. I'd never get to eat if I said that.

We had our plague masks in the console between the seats to put on when Joe came out with the food. The couple did not wear masks. Why would a girl not wearing pants wear a mask? They would live forever.

While camped out on the toilet doing my inadequate cleansing yesterday, I noticed we had a whole six pack of toilet cleaner under the sink. Meg and I make Costco runs out in the burbs, even though there's just the two of us now. We're bulking up to give us something solid in this just-in-case pandemic era. How long does a six pack of that stuff last? Will that toilet cleaner outlive us?

"Who said anything about torturing?" I said. I hated that word, undies—a little-kid word.

"Nah," I said. "She's got nothing. Nothing on under there."

"Maybe you should ask her," she said.

I sat on that for a second. I twisted in my seat to look back at the Spice Island door. It wasn't like Joe to not have our food ready. My favorite restaurant—how can you argue with a name like that? The closest we were ever going to get to an island of spice. We'd have to wear tie-dye to go to a Spice Island. I thought that'd get a smile out of Meg if I said it out loud. But just then Joe's cook stormed out the door in his stained apron and kept on walking.

Meg and I looked at each other. "Not good," we both said.

Even though most of the factories were gone, we still had bad air. Something about pollution stalling out above us like the dirt on that Charlie Brown kid—Piggy, or something. Why are they running Charlie Brown reruns in the comics? They weren't funny the first time.

"I'll go check," I said.

"You do that," she said.

I eased out of the car, a little woozy, light-headed, during the first summer of COVID. I leaned into the door while slamming it, and the young couple looked up again. They'd been kissing, damn it.

I wore khakis and a blue sports shirt. A uniform for guys like me for special outings. I liked the shirt because it never wrinkled. I guess they call it a golf shirt, but I do not golf. I am a lawn-care pro specializing in poison and fake green. I had dressed up for the hospital.

For a second, I paused between turning toward Spice Island or toward Romano's. I shuffled my feet in the gravel as if trying to kick up a spark, but I knew where I was going. I didn't need to know whether she had anything on under that shirt. We were hungry.

Single Room

Julie sat on the edge of her bed and stared at her thin fingers, imagining bones beneath pale skin, their fragile hinges. Her room was a narrow rectangle—bed, dresser, desk, bathroom—one of the few singles in Helton Hall. When she came back from study abroad in France, she didn't want anybody seeing her thin, naked body. Watching her sleep. Or not sleep. Asking what was wrong. She slipped in and out, barely noticed, a sliver, a slight irritation beneath the skin of the friendly, intimate dorm. It cost more than a double, but her worried parents gladly paid the difference.

Now, here was Jason, sprawled in her desk chair, grinning like a fool, talking about sex like a fool, like he knew something. He was the first person to enter her room all semester, not counting her RA, who poked her head in once or twice at the beginning, then gave up.

Back when they were sophomores, Jason was sleeping with Kate, who lived across the hall from Julie. Early one morning, Julie dashed out of the communal bathrooms in her underwear. It was usually safe that early, but as she neared her room, Kate's door opened, and out stumbled Jason. Little

Kate with the big boobs and shit for brains who stole Julie's hairbrush and could not be trusted. No turning back—Julie quickly squeezed by him into her room, burning under his blatant stare.

"You sure looked sexy," Jason marveled. As if such a thing were possible, given her present state. "Red bra and panties. Shiny red."

"I was half asleep. Seeing you woke me up." Julie smiled tightly, still trying to figure out what Jason was doing in her room. "A long time ago," she said.

A few weeks earlier, he'd started joining her in the student union where she sat with her tea and books. They had mostly talked about their philosophy class. Then last week, out of the blue, he had asked her to a concert on campus—Gemini, a mediocre one-hit-wonder rock band on a tour of small colleges throughout the Midwest. "It was a good hit, though," he'd told her. Out of the blue. Out of the blue, blue sky. And she had emerged from her cloud long enough to laugh. To say yes.

It was black now—out there, behind her drawn curtains. She reached over to yank them open a crack, imagining it would help her breathe. The loud music still buzzed in her ears like a pesky insect, and Jason was still there, also pesky. He'd invited himself in. She'd offered him tea. Tea. He was amused by that. Jason seemed amused by everything. His laughter seemed to Julie like a false wave he road on. It kept him on the surface. But she *needed* more surface, she knew. She needed to stop digging away at herself.

"Woke me up too," Jason said. Not touching his tea. Herbal, Julie's own mix. A long pause. Jason looked around the room, nodding as if everything confirmed something he knew all along. A lone shiny red apple sat on her empty desk. Everything else neatly stashed away. No cute or tacky posters on the wall. No scattered makeup or hair products. No open notebooks or dirty clothes. He picked up the apple and rubbed it between his hands. "Never been in a single before," he said. The pressure of focusing on him, of making ordinary speech, had exhausted her. Julie hoped the silence meant he would leave soon. But no—he had simply paused before asking the question that sent her spiraling every time someone asked it, down into the echoing cavern where she shouted, *hello, hello,* and no one answered.

"So, what happened? What happened to you?" He smiled, like it was a joke, or a riddle.

She bunched the simple, white chenille bedspread in her hands that had once been her grandmother's. It covered up her old girly, flowery one. She was always cold and needed them both. "Happened?" She tried to make her voice go flat, but it still seemed as shrill as a radio ad.

"You go to France for a semester, then you come back. You lose all this weight. You quit the sorority. You get a single. I mean . . ."

She didn't want to hear what he meant.

"The doctors thought I had ulcers." She turned on her robot voice. "Then they thought I was hypoglycemic. Then they thought I was a hypochondriac. I have trouble. I have trouble eating."

Jason paused. He tried to catch her eye, but she turned away. "You're anorexic?" Jason was thin himself, and tall. Handsome, everyone said, and he ran through girlfriends on a monthly basis. What was he doing here, Julie wondered again. He put the apple back on the desk.

"That's what they settled on," she said. It was what *she* had settled on—a way to slowly withdraw, disappear. Everybody said she was sealing herself off, but wasn't Jason Stark sitting in her room past midnight?

"I should take a picture of you to send home to my parents," she said with a bitter laugh, but then she felt tears rising, so she clammed up. She was pathetic. How had Paris leeched out all her color? Learning another language through immersion. People don't think about how you get immersed in yourself, alone in a foreign country.

"I should take a picture of *you* to send home. I think we both need evidence to call off the dogs." He brushed a tear away from her cheek with a thumb. It surprised her, how gentle. "What happened over there?" Then he said, right when she was beginning to imagine she felt something, "Somebody break your heart?"

Jason was suddenly beside her on the bed, putting his arm around her. No one had ever broken her heart. She thought she should stand up, move away, but she felt drained. She'd promised herself to eat that apple before she went to bed—a beautiful Red Delicious she'd picked up from a bowl in the cafeteria. The smell of that place made her nauseous now. She couldn't even eat an apple in there, at a table by herself—the Stick Girl, too good for the Alpha Thetas, too good for her old boyfriend, Mitch, and his studly jock friends. The cacophony of everyone eating and talking clattered in her head like the casual disasters of dropped silverware and breaking glass.

"Nobody broke my heart." She thought that sounded petulant—not the tone she was looking for. She was looking for disinterest. She knew she had it in her, that lack of interest. She depended on it to get through each day.

"You were one of the hottest ladies on campus—I don't mean you're ugly now—but . . ." That was it: he still had a crush on her old self. He fiddled with the zipper on his jacket. She had just about convinced him that the one he remembered was long gone. Maybe now he might be willing to leave. Maybe she should show him her plain white sagging cotton underwear just to finish him off.

"'Hot ladies,' Jason?" She shook her head. He wasn't a frat boy, but he surely was a boy. A boy, and proud of it.

"Hey, give me a break." He was standing now. "I'm trying to figure out how to act around girls when I'm not loaded. I thought you'd be a good place to start."

"Jason, I'm not a *place*," she said angrily. "Sit down . . . I didn't know." He hesitated. "Sit down and take off your damn jacket," she told him.

His smile made a quick return. "I'm sorry," he said. He looked like an innocent boy with that smile. Or a spoiled boy who could get away with anything. "You used to be a place," he said.

"What the hell does that mean?" She had to laugh, though. She could see he was joking, and that he was serious too. She used to be a place. She used to have substance. Now, she was a twig. A twig broken off a tree, a twig blowing in the wind. A twig that might never blossom into leaf again. That didn't know how.

"Yeah, I quit drinking. I was getting lost all the time and ending up with a lot of names I couldn't remember. . . . I remembered your name."

"You remember my underwear," she said.

"I remember what I remember," he said. She was going to roll her eyes, but he suddenly bent down and kissed her. Her lips were a dry sponge, but they met his. When he tried to pull her to him, to moisten her mouth with his tongue, she did not resist. She did not respond. He stopped.

"I'm sorry, Julie, but that's creepy. I feel like I kissed a ghost or something."

"It's not just you. It's everybody. Boys, girls—everybody." She leaned back on the bed until her spine cracked against the wall. "Ask Mitch." She was nearly shouting now. Why was she defending herself? She'd been over it all with her parents, the doctors.

"I don't have to ask anybody," Jason interrupted, "Christ, I remember watching you dance—you had some moves." Julie wouldn't dance at the concert, though Jason had repeatedly asked her to. The loud music bored her. Gemini played its one hit twice—they were old, gone to seed, running on fumes of empty volume.

"You going to eat this?" he asked, picking up the apple again, holding it up like a baseball, pretending to throw it. She would have to wash it again.

"I might get kicked out of the garden if I don't," she said. He started to say something, but stopped. He put the apple back on the desk.

Julie felt like her body would simply crumble into a pile of bones if she tried to dance. All she could manage was an awkward sway. She was so stiff that it hurt everywhere. Sometimes even walking was a struggle, mechanically kicking out each leg. Who had gone and stolen her grace? She was still young—that's what everyone kept telling her.

"Why did you ask me to the concert?" she asked.

"What?" Jason asked, though she knew he heard her. "Stand up," he said. "And let me look at you."

"What?" They were both going deaf in that small room.

"Never mind," he said. "Why did you come with me?"

"You wish you were at a party or something."

"I've been to enough parties," he said. "I just don't know what to do with the time. The time I used to spend on parties."

"You could study," she said. They both laughed.

"Yeah, there's that." He was double majoring in economics and philosophy. She knew he had another side, and she was half interested in seeing if she could find it. Maybe he was too. She knew she was getting too thin to even have another side.

She went to Paris as a French major, but her advisor said her French was worse when she returned. She'd switched to English because she'd always liked poetry, but now her voice was disappearing along with the rest of her, her body shrinking into a flat cartoon. Even her thought bubbles seemed blank.

Back before she met Mitch, she would've slept with Jason, just for the pure physical rush. Even though he seemed like an egotistical jerk, she had to admit he was handsome. She remembered the joyful rhythm of sex, the smooth, slick skin, but it was like a movie that had just ended—the lights flicked on in the theater, and all she could do now was squint as the picture faded. She remembered entering her room that morning he'd seen her, closing the door, leaning back against it, her body pulsing with shock and lust. Her roommate Jill, still asleep, buried under rumpled covers. Julie hit her with a pillow and told her what happened. Jill, who now treated her like a bad grade she didn't deserve.

One thing about Mitch—he had an athlete's endurance and grace. But when she returned from Paris and he was all over her, his pent-up lust longing to be sated, she was repulsed. Her body rigid as he pounded inside her. She had hoped seeing him again would snap her out of the spell she'd fallen into, wandering Paris streets like a zombie, but the zombie had returned with her, sapping all desire. They broke up two weeks into the new semester. He first assumed she'd found some romantic Frenchman, then asked if she was a lesbian. Everyone wanted an explanation.

In Paris, she'd been free to be someone new, to remake herself without the baggage of the old self. What an opportunity, everyone said. She herself couldn't wait to get away from that small college, Greek letters stamped on her T-shirt and an invisible map of the rest of her life traced on her forehead.

At the school in Paris, a converted Catholic convent, students from all over the world studied French. She remembered walking down a dark, damp street mined with dog shit, feeling none of the magic you were supposed to feel in Paris. And if she couldn't feel it in Paris, she must be lost, naive, sick, rigid, and dying in her young bones.

She had built it up in her mind: Paris for a semester. Great wine. Great food. Beautiful art. Sophistication. And yes, maybe a romantic Frenchman. In the small town in Northern Michigan where her father owned the hardware store, no one ever went to Detroit, much less Paris, but there she was. Her weekly hometown newspaper asked her to write a story. She never wrote a word, knowing they wouldn't be interested in something titled "How to Become a Ghost."

One day, a month after she arrived in Paris, she encountered a handsome man setting up a small carnival in a park near her dorm. He wore a tight, ribbed T-shirt, and his dark curly hair sprawled out from beneath a blue cap. Grease streaked his muscular arms. Early March, but the strong sun allowed her to imagine spring. She walked up and asked when the carnival was going to open. "When you kiss me," he said. It might have been a flirtatious comment, except for the look on his face—more than disinterest or rudeness. More than glower and bluster. It looked like pure hatred. The menace from his dark eyes staggered her. Her bad accent gave her away as American. "No," she said, trying quickly again, "When does it open?"

"Go away, stupid American girl," he said in English. He spat at her and grabbed his crotch, then turned quickly back to his work to make sure she understood. He didn't want a kiss.

Was she so windblown that one rude man on a street could stagger her? She had not even told this story to her therapist. It wasn't even enough to call a story. Her family seemed to think she must have been assaulted or raped. She couldn't tell them it had been such a small thing. She might have even given the man a kiss—robust, clean-cut, not like the scruffy carnies who passed through town working the midway at the county fair. It was like biting into a beautiful ripe apple and finding a worm.

Then it began. She stopped eating the wonderful crusty bread, the rich gooey cheeses. The other Americans in the program had bonded during the first week when Julie was still getting over jet lag and missing Mitch. She had tried to mingle, but mingling there had a whole new complicated structure. The city was enormous, the dorm overcrowded, and the school's extraordinary mix of languages disorienting. She withdrew into the small safe town of her tiny cell where nuns had lived for centuries. She crossed days off her calendar. In class, she refused to speak. She shopped by pointing and shrugging at impatient merchants. Her grades suffered. Her parents assumed she was just having too much fun.

This is what she'd become, and nobody liked it. It was like letting a lion out of its cage and the lion getting out and making an even smaller cage for itself, then locking itself in.

"I just found myself drinking more and more at every party. Like it was expected of me," Jason rambled on, "I treated some women pretty crummy."

"Is this what you want? To confess?" she asked. Jason had serious problems, Julie realized. And here he was trying to kiss the priest. "Is this your new way to pick up women?"

Her breasts were shrinking, her body turning into sharp, brittle angles. Was she killing herself? Her parents called nightly, and she gave them her empty news. She'd missed the call tonight. "Yes, I just ate an apple," she could've told them. She was staring at it on the desk.

Jason ran his hands through his longish blonde hair, then rested his elbows on his knees. "Maybe you're right. I mean, about confessing, not the picking up part. You're tuning me out just like my friends . . . I figured you must've stopped drinking too . . ."

"I did, but it's not just that, Jason. It's life. You're trying to simplify everything…" She could still taste his fat tongue. She swallowed the last of her tea, then took Jason's cup and set them both together on the shelf above her bed. Two empty cups. She felt like she might have a few things to say to him after all. "Who are you to come into my life and mock me with this sensitivity and confession shit? You'd still be talking, even if I turned into a ghost this very second." She dropped back onto the edge of the bed so hard she flinched as her tailbone hit the hard frame.

Jason didn't respond. Didn't rise to leave, to make her room safe again. Instead, he moved the desk chair closer. She bent over too, as if something was pushing them both down, elbows on knees, point to point. A football huddle—who was going to go out for the pass? Jason leaned his head forward till their foreheads touched at the hairline, bone to bone.

It was late. Julie was tired. Jason wasn't going anywhere, the sober pretty-boy, tired of his own good looks. His forehead felt cool against hers. She closed her eyes and sighed. "Okay," she said. Maybe she could teach him to starve.

Just a Crack

Alice opened the door just a crack, as if someone lurked behind her who she didn't want me to see.

"Is this a bad time?" I asked. "I thought . . ."

"You came," she said quickly, then yanked me inside for a long, hard kiss. It almost hurt.

"I didn't think I'd ever get to do that again," she said, finally pulling away and taking a breath. I put my fingers to my lips and felt her moisture there.

"Wow," I said. She smiled a little too wide. High on something, her eyes dilated. Drugs were at play—I wasn't sure which ones, though we'd never been selective. She had once stopped me from doing heroin with her and her friends. She went in the other room with them but would not let me in. I'd resented her for that. Then, later, I was grateful for that.

It'd been three years since I'd seen her. Two since I'd more or less straightened up. I was half straight, a dangerous place to be with that person, in that neighborhood, with our history.

I pulled her crookedly folded letter from my back pocket and held it up. "How could anyone not respond to a letter like this?"

She flushed—a blush? In that August heat, it could have been anything, even anger. She was dressed as if to go out—tight black short skirt, silky low-cut white blouse. Her long black straight hair sent off a glittery scent and sheen. For me, I thought, she dressed up for me. I wore black jeans and a pocket T-shirt—what she'd remember me always wearing.

Alice had written me an "I don't know if you'll ever read this and you can pretend you never received it" letter. I got it, read it, and here I was, at her small house on the East Side of Detroit on a street with five and a half houses left on it, their square punctuation breaking up the wild script of weeds and rubble. The city was planning to take down the half-house, she told me, but, with the huge backlog on tearing down abandoned houses, it could be years. The roof caving in on the remaining half drove the crackheads back out to roam the streets until they found another abandoned house to set up shop in. They would not have to go far, but there was nowhere left for them there on Edsel Street. I was a little rusty, not sure what she was on—not sure what anyone was on, everything laced with fentanyl, killing people with its random, deadly accuracy. People who thought they were getting something else.

We stood on the other side of the door. I felt the ragged, peeling paint against my back. I waited for her to lead me into the living room, but she seemed content to keep me in that corner, oblivious to the space around us. Me, in that tiny room of squalor, I didn't know what I was getting either.

Nothing to read anywhere, I noted quickly. She'd always been reading something. I remembered sitting in the eye doctor's office when I was a kid, waiting after getting drops, my blurry eyes unable to read the old *Highlights* magazines scattered over the low table in the waiting room. I knew all the games and puzzles were already filled in anyway. Did she see it that way now?

We had become friends over books back in high school. Both of us into the Beats. Their rough scruff and rants allowed us to scrape off the glue of our sticky, stifling classrooms where we read old poems full of *thees* and *thous*. We invented a secret code of obscene gestures and created new meanings for mundane words—our lockers were our coffins. We were the living dead. All that posturing seemed quaint now, ten years later.

"Can we sit down?" I asked. I had nothing except the letter, a fucking beautiful letter in her perfect tiny script that got smaller as it went on, trailing off into squiggles I could not decipher. She was someone who could've carved the Bible on a bar of soap. A coin. A grain of ice. A tab of acid.

She turned and led me into the shabby living room—a basic couch, coffee table, chair set-up. It reminded me of my grandparents' furniture in their house on Brinket that'd been a few blocks from here until we abandoned it to crumble in on itself like so many others. We left that furniture behind. I briefly had the crazy idea that this might be their furniture, salvaged and rescued before the demolition. The same old tangled, green fringe hung from the bottom of the couch.

She spread her arms out in front of the couch as if revealing it. "Sit here," she said. She plopped down, and I plopped down. We sank deeper than I had anticipated.

"Hey, before I kiss you again, are you living alone?" I asked. An electric Harley-Davidson clock buzzed on the wall above us.

Her letter was about us, everything she remembered, and missed—how we'd grown from casual pals into fierce lovers. Nostalgic, for sure, and I was all in favor of some clean, simple, burnished nostalgia for back when we were wanna-be rebels, before that rebellion washed away in our self-manufactured storms.

"I didn't know if you were attached, married or what," she said. "It was a shot in the dark. I was aiming for that old moon we used to have. I was and am—well, you could tell from the letter, couldn't you?—extremely unhappy. It was an impulse, that letter, but I had no stamps, so the sending of it was not an impulse."

"So, the answer is, no?"

She gave me that crazed grin and pulled me down on top of her. Up close, her hair, less glossy, almost crackled with hair spray, but maybe I was just shining up the rearview mirror. I ran my hands through that hair, splaying it gently on both sides of her almond face. Once, a lover found Alice's high school graduation photo in my dresser and burned it. That's how beautiful she was. She didn't need all that makeup. She didn't need the short, shimmering skirt.

Soon, we were naked, or half naked, like that half a house. There was no shelter for anyone on the stained couch.

...

Despite our urgent intentions, the sex was awkward and rushed. The guy would be back around seven, and he would not be pleased to find me there. Six-thirty when she told me that, according to Harley-Davidson.

It felt like she'd changed the channel on the TV to the Canadian station, something obscure with an accent I could not translate. The guy—she wouldn't say a name. Her exposed breasts beaded up and trickled with sweat. I felt it gathering at my hairline. The windows painted shut. The room needed a window unit, or at least a fan.

"I don't remember ever fucking during the day," I said. We'd barely said a word about the last three years. Maybe we had to get the sex out of the way first, though now we'd lost all time to catch up. I'd brought a couple of condoms, but only used one. Even one was presumptuous, but that letter—it shook me out of the convenient new high-rise apartment off the expressway in suburban Philadelphia, the comfortable dead-end job as a tutor for rich kids taking the SAT, the meal delivery service, the reliable Toyota, and the smug assumption of marriage that my live-in girlfriend, Mona, and I shared. Maybe the *all that* of my teens and early twenties wasn't over with, and it was still possible to stop the train and jump back into overfertilized weeds blooming into surreal pathways guaranteed to get me lost.

"All we ever did was fuck," she said. She made no effort to move, get dressed. Time watered down by drugs, or drowned by them.

We'd been lovers off and on starting in high school. People were going steady and asking each other to the prom and accidentally getting pregnant, and what were we doing? Night stalkers, we flashed each other secret signals and rendezvoused between anonymous buildings or tall trees. Our lust drew us together into small but potent explosives that obliterated other commitments, relationships, evaporating them into a smoky haze.

The sex became almost a way of saying hi. When I moved to Philly, they might have hired her too, but neither of us were sure we wanted that. She had this guy at the time, and things were complicated, she said. It was no big deal, we told each other. Our comfort zone had always been as a thing on the side. Too close, and we'd start to burn each other up.

Two states away, we could still do what we'd always done, couldn't we? But she'd slowly and impossibly disappeared. Until now. Not that I'd scoured the earth for her. In Philly, Mona had helped me get half straight and was working on the other half. The other half—that was my problem.

•••

"Is there a problem?" she asked

"I didn't say there was a problem. It's just so . . . so crazy." The ruined state of the house was asserting itself. The piled dishes, the torn rug, the dingy coating of dust on everything. The clock.

"Who is this guy?"

She shook her head. That smile again. It seemed pasted on, on the verge of coming off. A drug mask.

"Hey, just tell me if he has a gun." The clock. I pointed above us.

I half-meant it as a joke, but she sat silent as I waited. "You'll take it the wrong way," she finally said.

"What other way is there to take it? I should leave."

"What happened? I can't even remember," she asked.

"We're living two states apart," I said. "One was okay, two was too many."

I stood up, pulled my pants up, and zipped up. We'd never had expectations beyond the moment. Not ones we talked about. Though we talked about almost everything else.

"I don't have one picture of you," she said.

"We never took pictures." I coughed out a laugh. "It was always dark."

"I need one now," she said.

I held my shirt, ready to pull it over my head. She held her phone. "No shirt, please," she said, quickly snapping.

I pulled the letter out of my pants pocket again. "I forgot how beautiful your handwriting is."

"So did I," she said. "I couldn't type it. I didn't know where to find you." The letter had been forwarded from my parents' old address. My mother had put it on the dresser in the spare room of her apartment when I came home for Thanksgiving. She'd just kept it for my next visit home instead of forwarding it further on. Nothing was urgent for her since my father had died. Time had taken on an odd arbitrary nonlinear function.

"So, he has a gun."

"Yeah, but look where I live," she said.

"Look," I said. "What are you on that makes you live here?" I didn't want to come down on her. I had no high horse to climb off of, just a nice car parked out on that ravaged street. "This is messed up. How do you even know what you're taking anymore with fentanyl everywhere?"

I knew how that would come at her—like a stern parent, a school counselor, a social worker—but we'd squandered the time for subtlety. She was putting herself back together, ignoring me. I glanced again at the green couch, the frayed fringe, a stain that I might have just made.

"Why are you here?" I nearly shouted. "You're the smartest person I know. How are you making a living?" She'd put herself through Wayne State waitressing, then got a job managing a small chain of coney dog places, last I'd heard.

"Do you really want to get into that?" she said.

No, I did not. Yes, I did. I held her arms in my hands like we were waiting for the music to start so we could dance.

"You're the smart one," she said. "You figure it out."

"Why did you write?" I said slowly, as if typing out each word. "I'm not so smart. You fooled me."

The clockface gave me ten minutes before the man with the gun showed up. What did she owe him? Money? Sex?

"I wanted to see if you'd come." Her eyes welled with tears that fell off her bent-over face. We weren't going to kiss again. I pulled open the door and rushed out.

I know I glossed over living with Mona in Philly, and I have no excuses. I should never go back to Detroit. I should parachute down to my mother's apartment in the suburbs rather than drive those streets again where I imagined I had nothing to lose.

I thought about waiting just to see him, but I knew *just* might not be the end of it. Despite not having a gun. Because not having a gun. Because how could the smartest person I knew be selling themselves for drugs, which was my best guess.

You can ask why I went to see her, and I can pretend I know. Someday, she may write me again, and I can't say I won't write back. I had her phone number. A phone number. I gave her a beat-up business card from my wallet. She took it into the bathroom and did not return with it. Did she memorize it and swallow it like a spy?

We'd had another goodbye fuck. But it had seemed crude, without passion. I started the car and idled, watching the exhaust plume in the air behind me. I turned the radio on, then off again. My forehead kissed the steering wheel. The few cars parked on Edsel leaked despair from their rusty, ragged edges. One Bondo job sat up on blocks, waiting to be repainted. Another had a white door where a blue one should be. In Detroit you could always scavenge parts for your car if you weren't fussy, and no one on that street looked very fussy.

Goodbye fucks—I never imagined that Alice and I would stop having them. The next day I'd head back to Philly, where I might have another one with Mona, who was tired of me glossing things over. Dominoes without dots, no way to win.

Another car had pulled up behind me, also idling. Tinted windows, luxury sedan, in good shape. I knew so little. What had become of us?

I was in danger of going nonlinear myself until someone in that dark car flashed its lights, leaned on its horn. I was clearly taking up the wrong space on that half-abandoned street. I imagined looking up and over at Alice's house and seeing only half a house, but instead I looked straight ahead. I didn't want to get into all that. I put it into drive and pulled away.

The Flying Wallendas

Karl Wallenda developed some of the most amazing acts like the seven-person chair pyramid. The Flying Wallendas continued performing those acts until 1962. That year, while performing at the Shrine Circus at Detroit's State Fair Coliseum, the front man on the wire faltered and the pyramid collapsed. Three men fell to the ground, killing two of them. Karl injured his pelvis, and his adopted son, Mario, was paralyzed from the waist down.

A number of branches have fallen off the Wallenda tree since 1962. My own tree, the Sokolowski tree, was struck by lightning. Our old man, Slick Rick—that's what our mother called him—keeled over from a heart attack while he was in the middle of drawing that tree, his hand squiggling a stray angled line across the whole thing to connect me and Peggy, my brother Randy's ex-wife. Peggy lives with me now.

Yeah.

•••

I stood outside the patched, faded circus tent at the State Fairgrounds waiting for Peggy to come back from parking the car in the rutted, dirt lot. I know the circus isn't what it used to be back in the Flying Wallendas days, but all circuses have that smell: exotic animal shit, cigars from Swampbreath, Louisiana, melting makeup from Buttercup, Missouri, and roadie scum from every federal prison in the good ol' US of A.

•••

The Wallendas were always big in Detroit. In the constant free-fall off of our own economic, political, social high wires, we identified with their tragedies, searching for the elusive net to stop our endless collapse, or wishing for the fatal impact against hard ground.

Randy once got a concussion trying to jump from one bunk bed to the next and crashing to the floor in between. Back then, we just said he got his bell rung. Randy had a hard head, everybody knew. Nothing could hurt Randy, flying Randy. He carried himself that way, leading with the jaw, daring the world to mess with him. And I did. I hurt him.

I don't want to be all about justifying what I did, but I will say that I didn't want to do it. Why steal your brother's wife, knowing all the hassle that's coming down the line? It's like cutting the damn tightrope on yourself. Randy was already cutting that rope, but with a duller knife than mine. Tight wire, really. I don't know when they stopped using ropes. Lots of things I don't know.

•••

"What are you waiting for, you idiot? I thought you were getting us good seats," Peggy said as she hustled up, out of breath. We'd been living together three years and two-and-a-half months, and she didn't think twice about calling me an idiot. I didn't mind. And if I ignored her, she didn't seem to mind that either.

"Watch this guy," I said. An ancient toothless man with Vaselined lips was eating fire at a tiny sawdust ring set up near the entrance to the big tent. Another man, who may have been his brother, was barking through a megaphone powered by spit and flashlight batteries.

"Buy your tickets, see more inside," he repeated endlessly while his brother grabbed torch after torch from a rack, lit them with his lighter, and put them out in his mouth. Like he was working an assembly line, and those torches, once he swallowed the fire, would become car parts.

Peggy stopped for five seconds to watch, then grabbed a ticket from my hand and brushed past me. "Meet me inside."

Peggy and I have an understanding. If you can come to an understanding with someone, you can live with just about anything. I lost my driver's license three months ago and won't get it back for three more. Too many demerits, points, whatever they call them. We accumulate points, then we have to wait to make them disappear. I didn't wait long enough.

•••

Sawdust, another great circus smell. Sawdust—work getting done, something new emerging, rising. Sure, it's also used to clean up shit and piss, but it works. Light, fluffy, piney. In heaven, they probably have sawdust on the ground.

•••

"You always wait too long or not enough," Peggy liked to say. I overlapped with Randy, is what she's talking about. He got furloughed at Ford's, and when his unemployment ran out, he drove to Texas to look for work in the oil fields—it was a thing back then during one of the many downturns in the auto industry. Detroit newsstands carried Texas Sunday papers with their thick help wanted sections, and unshaven, hungover, laid-off autoworkers waited in line to buy them. Their kids, Roscoe and Bailey, were in school, so they stayed put with Peggy while Randy drove around Texas in his pickup with Michigan plates until he literally got into an accident, I kid you not, with another pickup with Michigan plates—a matter of Randy leading with his head again is the short version of that.

With Randy gone, time stretched out long enough for Peggy and I to be having sleepovers before he came back. I don't mean to be coy—it did almost feel that innocent at first. It started one night when I fell asleep on her couch. She kissed me on the forehead and went to bed. Maybe I wasn't quite asleep. I got up to take a piss in the middle of the night and ended up in bed with her.

Who would do that to their own brother?

•••

I help people cheat on their taxes. Ever since we got three casinos in Detroit to stem the tide of our green dollars dulling up the bright wallets of the wise Canadians in Windsor, I've been accidentally and illegally rolling in it. Rolling in my own shit. Do elephants do that, like dogs, like I'm doing now? Or is that rolling in dead animals? It's instinctual, just like jumping from one bed to another, eh, Randy? I became a big fan of instinct after Peggy and I got together—my explanation to anyone who would listen, who did not want to kill me.

•••

Fire-eater. That's what I do. People bring me their fires, and I eat them. Oh, it burns the soul a little, but I'm well paid. Three casinos, and I've got a pal in each. A pal in Canada too. If I had a friend at the IRS, maybe I'd have a leader for the band, but, as it stands, I'm the leader, taking all the risks. They call me Mr. Phony Baloney, which would be my clown name if I were a clown.

Randy knows about it—the dirty business that's strictly business, not personal. He hasn't turned me in by now, so I don't imagine he will. Randy's not a friend of the court, if you know what I mean—he wouldn't want to get all palsy with them due to how he got by once he returned from Texas and started freelancing.

•••

Most people had shuffled inside the tent. The musty canvas exuded the sweat and damp dirt of endless putting ups and taking downs, even from where I stood. Add that to the list of circus comforts.

The twins stared at me. It looked like I'd waited long enough. "Show starts in two minutes," Mr. Megaphone barked at me in his gravelly old-dog smoker's voice. He didn't need the megaphone.

They both had shaved heads, though I don't imagine much shaving needed to be done. They looked like twins doing the Munch "Scream." I heard he painted *The Scream* a whole bunch of times. You'd think once would be enough. The two of them looked like they'd kill themselves if I didn't go inside in two minutes.

•••

Brother Screams. I spent my early years trying to impress Randy. Top-bunk brothers, sixteen months apart. The other two, Reggie and Miles, on the bottom bunks. They both signed the "You're Dead to Us" letter. They passed it around the family, then around the old neighborhood, collecting signatures. They attached it to a rock and threw it through my picture window, old-school style. After that, we kind of lost touch.

I imagine they debated hiring a hit man, but nobody wanted to spend the money to end my suffering. My family's full of cheap-ass motherfuckers, myself included. When you get the skim money, you don't want to get caught with cream on your face, so I developed the habit of not doing any show-off spending—well, hardly any.

Peggy and I are going to buy a place on an island someday. I want to get off this island of exile here in Detroit. We may as well go to the Caribbean and get some sunburn out of the deal. I dream of just the two of us deserted on an island like in the cartoons. Just us and a coconut tree. We wouldn't be writing "Save Us" in the sand.

•••

Behind the two old men, lightning began to crackle in the distance above the old fairground grandstand where they once had horse races. They're trying to kill the traveling circuses, but in small towns around the country, despite cable TV, the internet, all the streaming, people come out to smell a world different from the odorless one they live in. A world with nothing subtle about it. A world where you get all the jokes and don't miss a trick.

Thunder rumbled. Or maybe it was the crowd murmuring under the big top. I handed my ticket to a woman in a spangled leotard. She wore false eyelashes so enormous she looked stoned, ready to nod out. "Stay alert, sister," I said. "Storm on the horizon."

"Yeah, whatever," she said, tearing my ticket in half, throwing both halves in a battered wooden box.

Though the tent was only half full, Peggy had picked lousy seats. Front row, so the clowns would pick on us, but I joined her. Of course, I joined her. We were Siamese twins for adultery.

···

Our father loved to take us to the Shrine Circus at the fairgrounds. He got discount tickets from a guy at the plant. He wasn't a shriner himself—our father in a fez? Just the thought makes me laugh. The old man never blinked when Peggy and I officially joined forces—he was rolling over in his grave instead.

Slick Rick packed the five of us in the station wagon every year. He'd buy us cotton candy, popcorn, even the souvenir coloring book. One year—I know this sounds like a small thing—the vendor accidentally gave me two copies of the thin coloring book that had stuck together. Randy told our dad, but he let me keep them both. "It's not fair," Randy whined all the way home till Slick Rick reached around at a red light and cuffed him. I'll always remember what he said: "It's just a goddamn coloring book!"

···

The circus acts lumbered in and out of the sawdust. I won't bother with the play-by-play. The front row allowed me to look the wise elephants in the eye and feel their calm. Peggy leaned her head on my shoulder, and the clowns mostly left us alone, so the show was pleasant in a predictable way. At least until it got unpredictable. Peg doesn't lean her head on my shoulder much anymore, though it's only been three years. Maybe if we set up a tent in the backyard and hung out in there, she'd lean into me more. And me into her.

•••

The most famous clown moment came on "Bozo's Showtime"—he filmed live every afternoon and Saturday morning in a studio across the river in Canada. We got a Canadian station on our TVs in Detroit, channel 9. Bozo's audience of kids competed in games, and he gave away prizes and did magic tricks even we could figure out. Canada had Bozo, and they had studio wrestling. Then, later, a lower drinking age, full nude dancing, and casinos. We had Canada envy, though we did not like their funny-colored money with the queen's stuck-up mug on it. It was worth less than ours.

So, this kid's playing Bozo's Treasure Chest, where you try to win a shitload chest of toys by tossing three ping pong balls in a barrel. The Treasure Chest! The grand prize! We set up a bucket in the basement at home and practiced, just in case we got the call to be on *Bozo's Showtime*. The kid got the first two, then missed the third.

Bozo says, in a friendly Canadian Bozo kind of way, "You're never a loser on 'Bozo's Showtime,' you're just an almost-winner!"

Everybody wanted to be on Bozo until a certain age, then nobody wanted to be on Bozo. I think this kid was in the littoral zone of Bozo.

He flips Bozo off and says, "Climb it, Clowny."

And Bozo says, "That's a Bozo no-no."

Or so I heard. We all heard. But no one I know actually saw the show. It aired live, and they taped over the tapes back then. It's possible that it never even happened.

•••

"Did you ever want to be on Bozo?" I asked as Peggy drove us home in my spotless Impala. I used to drive it over to Belle Isle by the aquarium, with its nice view of Canada across the river, to wash and wax it—a custom in the city, to show off both your car and your love of it.

Nobody seemed to treat their wives that well, did they, Randy? While it was true that he'd overextended his stay in Texas, and, as his brother, I knew about his own wandering around in that big state of marital shenanigans, of which I have never told Peggy, I do not offer excuses. Slick Rick taught us to suck it up—whatever it was that he deemed needed sucking up.

"Everybody wanted to be on Bozo," she said. "Climb it, Clowny," she said.

•••

"Maybe we should shave our heads like those two clowns out front," I said to Peggy.

"I didn't see any clowns out front," she said. No smoking in the big top. Peggy was scratching her fingers against the splintery portable grandstand. I grabbed her hands and held them to keep her steady.

"I mean the fire-eating Scream Brothers."

"The bald buskers? We could be The Screams."

"Yeah, that's what I was thinking." Peggy and me, our minds were in sync. We could leave out large parts of conversation and still understand each other. We had to leave out large chunks of just about everything—otherwise, we'd just be a couple of sin-eaters without time for anything else. It was a wonder our hair hadn't fallen out on its own.

Thunder rumbled closer outside the tent. It got quiet inside, and we could hear the moaning wind thudding against canvas.

•••

Roscoe and Bailey stayed with us one weekend a month. They called me Uncle Daddy as a joke. While I appreciated the cynical humor of that, it got old seeing them slouch in the door with their backpacks and greet me that way every month. They were too cool to get interested in the circus, to get invested in a new father figure. They were climbing on their own teenaged high wires, confident their joysticks would put them back up there after they fell.

Traveling circuses are getting hit by the animal-rights folks. The big cats, the elephants. Next, they're going to be protesting clown cruelty. Cruelty is a way of life, the law of the jungle. You take them out of the jungle, and yeah, maybe they're a little bored, but there's a big difference being bored and being dead (nobody carrying protest signs out in the jungle). Where's your middle ground? My whole life I've been falling into the in-between. Ripping off the government gives me pleasure. Living with my brother's ex-wife, on the other hand—well, it also gives me pleasure. With sadness mixed in. Nothing to haggle over because Peggy holds the cards. Sadness is the cage.

•••

"What's the point of having wild animals if we can't tame them?" Peggy said.

"By the way, climb it, Clowny," Peggy said again. She liked the alliteration. "That's a Bozo no-no," Peggy said. She liked the rhyme. My Peg, the poet.

•••

Or, maybe I'd be a ringmaster. Though they all seemed to be blowhard dandies.

"Am I a blowhard dandy?" I asked Peggy.

"Only on your better days," she said.

"Some days we sound like an old bickering married couple," I said.

"We're not bickering," she said.

We come close to talking about her years with Randy, but we always veer away from the crash zone onto some convenient back road.

"We're not married either," I said.

The ringmaster twirled his long microphone cord like the lion tamer's whip. I could do that. Snap! Snap!

•••

Power went out in the big top, but nobody fell, nobody got mauled, nobody died. Yet something happened.

The storm blew over, as storms always do, leaving behind random damage and infinite ways of rebuilding. In the dark tent, Peggy and I held each other close and waited. Kids in the crowd had purchased glow sticks, and in that darkness, the red and green sticks arced slowly through the air or held perfectly still, as if humbled by the greater light outside flashing close, closer.

Rain throbbed against the tent, battering the thick canvas, and the giant poles swayed. Thunder crashed and dashed, and lightning jerked giant shadows onto the walls.

The fire-eater with the megaphone—or his brother—spoke from very close by, though I couldn't make him out in the smudged blackness of shadows.

"Do not panic," he said, "Please remain in your seats. Do not stand. Do not push. Do not run."

Those who had risen sat back down. Their rustling settled like an ocean wave receding.

•••

We could hear carneys outside shouting instructions and curses, and the clinking thump of sledgehammers against the giant tent stakes, pounding them in deeper, though I felt anchorless in the storm's waves, no firm ground beneath us.

•••

In their backstage cages hidden behind canvas, big cats growled and roared— even their breath bled into the crowd without amplification. Or, rather, with the amplification of darkness and human fear and silence.

"Can you imagine . . ." I started to say, and Peggy put her other hand against my mouth to silence me, the most intimate of gestures. I felt sudden lust in that musky darkness, in that comfortable hell.

•••

Last year, they canceled the State Fair entirely. You wouldn't think a state could just cancel its fair. Look at the big whoopla out in Iowa every four years, politicians forced to eat corn dogs and deep-fried Oreos, sucking it up for the corn lobby.

Politicians killed the fair. A money-loser in a state bleeding money after the economy collapsed yet again, reliable as a tent in a storm. Detroit's a gambler's town, and we know the house always wins. You can get hot once in a while, when people start buying cars again for no clear reason, but you know—you *know*—it's just temporary.

The state wants to redevelop the fairgrounds. The giant stove—the "World's Largest"—burned down a few years back, and if that wasn't a sign to cash in your chips, then fuck you, mister. The stove weighed fifteen tons and stood twenty-five feet high. Built in 1893. We used to be the Stove City, not the Motor City. I'm a student of history and signs, which is why I no longer gamble myself.

•••

I never apologized to Randy, not wanting to be a hypocrite, in addition to being a thief, an adulterer, and all what else. We haven't spoken. Our silence has no hope in it. When their kids come and go, my eyes meet his through windshields, through screens, and all is numb—the numbness after a blow.

Is it better to be dead to them or dead to me?

•••

"Were you scared?" I asked Peggy as she drove us home, my feet restlessly pushing phantom pedals in the passenger seat. "In the storm?"

"A little," she said, glancing over as she turned onto the freeway off of Eight Mile Road. I needed to know she was scared too. "Hey, old man," she said, "When are we going to buy that island?"

"It's not an island. It's a house on an island," I said.

•••

Karl Wallenda once said, "Life is being on the wire, everything else is just waiting."

The only time I walked on the wire was with Peggy. The rest of my life, I've been selling programs and coloring books, cotton candy and snow cones, cheap felt pennants attached to foot-long pencils to wave on behalf of the country of circuses.

•••

You know how the Wallendas became the Flying Wallendas? One time after some of them fell, a newspaper guy wrote that they were so graceful, even while falling, that it looked like they were flying.

•••

We'll never get married—that would take away the net. Or, would it give us a net? Novelty wears off. The earth settles, and you settle with it into a subtle slump. Peggy's forty-three and I'm forty-five. We both did a big bad thing while we had the chance. I won't say everybody should risk ruining their lives, but a lot of us should. Karl kept trying till he was seventy-three.

Earth settling versus the foot on the wire. Addiction versus faith. Love versus the next best thing. Maybe our wire wasn't so high off the ground, but if you don't look down, you could be as far up as you want to be.

•••

My wife, Ruthie, died after a long battle with cancer. People always talk about "battling" cancer, but watching her long, drawn-out demise, it seemed to me that cancer always had all the weapons. Sure, the doctors pumped her full of poison drugs, but if it was a battle, they were shooting cap guns while cancer was dropping bombs. At the end, she was mostly dazed by sedation. We lasted thirteen years, not knowing any better, dazed by our own sedation. We'd agreed not to have kids, but when I was there in the hospital with her, she said maybe we should have. Slick Rick told me that not having kids was the one smart thing I'd done. Slick Rick, in his chair on top of the high-wire pyramid. I don't use losing Ruthie as an excuse for what I did—with Peggy—to

Randy. Or, maybe I do. It created a permanent weight imbalance in my own personal pyramid that maybe I took advantage of, just letting everything fall, not caring about the people I took down with me.

•••

When we were kids, Randy and I used to walk across Eight Mile Road to the fairgrounds to catch the bus to Tiger Stadium. My Aunt Tina got arrested at that bus stop for soliciting an undercover officer in what was a clear misunderstanding, given that Tina was sixty-eight. We're all undercover, is what I think.

When I think of Randy, it's all childhood stuff. Bunkbed memories.

"I was never the same after that concussion," he used to joke after forgetting something or remembering something no one else remembered. We used to lay on the top bunks across from each other, up in the air. Sometimes we'd look at each other and just laugh for no reason. When do we stop laughing for no reason?

•••

Peggy managed an office-supply store until it went under in the transition from paper to computers. She is now principal of a middle school in Detroit. She helped expose corruption in the system of office-supply acquisition due to knowledge from her previous job. You take what you learn and apply it to the next time around, right? She knows and doesn't know what I do. One more reason not to get married. We file separately.

•••

I was always attracted to her, even at their wedding. I was not the best man. I do believe or half-believe in animal attraction. For years, I avoided her—the pull of her. It was only with Randy in Texas—he finally came back when he found out—that the wall collapsed and we fell into each other. Cain slew Abel—I'm glad he didn't slay me.

•••

That night, the Magnificent Montoya Family used a net—a trapeze and high-wire combo act, a bow to the economics of circuses. They seemed too relaxed and smiley up there. They could at least pretend to be in danger. If somebody missed catching their arms, they just fell down like it was all planned. At the end of the performance, right before the power went out, they all casually tumbled down into the net. It seemed like the most dangerous part of the act—that they might land on top of each other.

It's tough when your signature move is one that killed people. Famous for dying, that's not on my list. If my parents and their five kids performed the seven-person chair pyramid, they'd be throwing me off, not Slick Rick.

Peggy and I never fit into the symmetry of that pyramid.

•••

I don't often remember dreams, but this one haunts me: I tumble down into the net, my family sprawled around me—my brothers and sister, my parents. No sign of Peggy. We're bouncing on the net, moving toward each other, everything gentle, as if the ocean is caressing us together again. Where is Peg? Did she miss the net? Then I fall through the net. It doesn't look like I could, but somehow I do. The truth is, we're all still walking around on this earth, or buried beneath it.

I don't put a lot of stock in dreams. I'm what they call a practical guy. "Not a sensitive bone in your body," Peggy once told me in what I took as an admiring way.

"What about my funny bone," I said, and we laughed.

"What about my Achilles heel?" we laughed again.

"What about . . ." but I could not think of another thing.

•••

Mario Wallenda, paralyzed from the waist down at twenty-one, made it till seventy-four and spent his life working in a contact lens factory in Florida, outliving his father Karl, who was blown off the wire at seventy-three. Why was Karl still up there?

Did Mario take satisfaction in outliving the old man who'd put him on the wire in the first place, just a kid really? How did Mario feel, looking up at the rest of the family from his chair for all those years? Relieved he'd never have to do it again? His parents even got married on the wire. I do! I do! Is there a mile-high club for tight-ropers?

Karl Wallenda, caught falling—the photographers were ready. Peg, are we still on the wire, or are we perpetually falling?

•••

Was Randy the fire-eater, or was I? When he came back from Texas high on speed and rage, breaking down the door, I thought for sure he was going to shoot me, or at least hit me with the baseball bat in his hand, but *he* just told me to get out. I looked at Peggy—she nodded, and I left. For one electric minute we were in the same room together—the living room of their tiny house in Warren less than a mile from where we grew up. The boys in their room—awake, I'm sure, due to the shattered glass, the splintering wood, their father breaking into his own house—did not emerge and have never emerged to discuss what happened.

•••

I have autographs of Karl and Mario and other Wallendas in my collection. I have a copy of the newspaper from the day after the accident, blaring headlines, dramatic photos. Brittle now, so I handle it gently. I can't explain the strange comfort it gives me as I fall.

•••

If I was on the high wire, I'd use a net. A good, strong one. When I watch someone up there, I forget whether there's a net or not after a while. It's the balancing that thrills me, not the death defying, since none of us really defy death.

"These are my people," I shouted to Peggy, gesturing up toward the Montoya family with both hands to make her laugh. Is it simpler to make someone laugh or to make someone hate you? Limbo is the state of in-between, buried under the Detroit River between Michigan and Canada. We want to find the lighted exit signs and leave limbo. Limbo is hell spelled differently.

•••

I love circuses because I love metaphor.

To go graceful while falling. To be graceful while waiting.

•••

I know it's hard to sympathize with someone whose life ambition has been to say, "Climb it, Clowny" to—to anyone, really. I'm not asking for sympathy, but a truce. To be not-dead to them before I die. I'm asking, but no one knows I'm asking. If Peggy dies first—when either of us dies, really—they might take the survivor back. Any trick that requires human sacrifice can only be done once. All the other tricks go on daily. Life is a pyramid scheme.

•••

One of the brothers clicked on a flashlight, trembling with improvisation in the darkness. "Now, we will witness the talents of Great Wilhelm the fire-eater. He shined that thin rope of light on his brother standing nearby. Wilhelm flicked his lighter, and the show began. So quiet we could hear the hiss of flame extinguished. Peggy's hand rested warm and slick in mine. I knew she desperately wanted to make a smaller flame, retreat to the steadiness of a pilot light.

Lighter fluid in a dark, full tent? They were breaking all the rules. Darkness has no rules. If you cannot see the net, there is no net.

All I know is that in the dark, hushed silence of the battered, swollen tent, we watched fire disappear.

Corrections

Hank swooped up I-75 past Rosa Parks Boulevard near where his favorite Detroit landmarks—Tiger Stadium, the Stroh's Brewery, the giant Goodyear Odometer—had been abandoned or destroyed. The odometer counted the number of cars built each year. How many, how few? The blank, unlit sign unnerved him. The tingling sting of anger welled up like a reverse splinter emerging from his skin. Why was he coming home for one more funeral? Reggie "Roof" Rakowski this time, shot in his own front yard in a drive-by. Reggie had a mouth on him and some history in his back pocket, but hell, once you're past forty, it was time to put the guns away and play nice. Why couldn't he mail in condolences at this point?

It'd been a few years since Hank moved down to Toledo for a job with Correct Corp., one of those private prison firms springing up across the country. He didn't know as many of the inmates as he did at the federal pen up in Milan, and he liked it that way. Though he was still obliged to return for occasions like these due to Toledo's proximity to Detroit—funerals, weddings, and the occasional dirty work his old biker crew demanded of him. A Marine for life, a Trojan Warrior for life, and a Wayne State graduate for life. How those three things fit together blurred like his drunken tattoos from Vietnam.

He got off at the Eight Mile exit and drove past the row of topless bars and cheap motels right off the ramp—places where they knew him as Phil during his alias bouncer days. He'd been engaged to a dancer at the Booby Trap—Robin, not her real name either—and she was ten years older than what she'd said, and he wanted to have kids someday, so that didn't work out.

Hank was more of a chump than he would ever admit. Despite his size—six-feet, four-inches tall, and 290 pounds, according to his physical for Correct Corp.—and his college degree, he had a strange gullibility that revealed itself at crucial moments to damage his life: personal, professional, financial. His father abandoned his mother before he was even born, but Hank had kept the secret hope alive that a man might come up to him some day and introduce himself as his father. His mother never remarried—never even dated, as far as Hank knew—and would not speak of the father, which allowed Hank to concoct various reunion scenarios as he lay in his tiny room in Riverside Projects on the East Side listening to the banging against walls and down from the ceiling that punctuated daily life in Riverside.

He pulled into the Hi-Fi station and filled his pickup. A big truck for a big man. He still had the Harley, but he wasn't pulling it out for a November ride up I-75. His friend Blue Dog worked the bulletproof glass box in the middle of the pumps, selling cheap gas and expensive cigarettes to the huddled masses, with a side business selling drugs, which made the bulletproof cage problematic at times and essential at others.

"Dog," Hank called out. Blue Dog looked up at him with glazed desperation.

"Lump, my man—up for the funeral? Good times in the city, my friend." Without being asked, he put his spare set of keys on the bulletproof carousel and wheeled it around to Hank. When in town, he slept on Blue Dog's couch. Blue Dog, like Hank, a lifelong bachelor. Though, unlike Hank, he had resigned himself to watching porn, giving up entirely on the real thing. The last time he'd been with a hooker, she told him to go take a shower and come back, and instead of showering, he upgraded his computer to cut down on the buffering.

"How'd that dumbass get shot shoveling snow? That ain't right."

"That's what the brotherhood is saying. Can't a man sell a few pills without getting his head blown off?"

A gust of wind from a passing semi plowed past Hank, and he turned his head away. Inside the box, Dog did not react. Hank pawed the keys into his cold, clumsy hands. He already had a bad feeling. His Glock sat holstered under his leather car coat. Funerals begot funerals.

"And this is affecting your business, how?" Hank asked.

"Same supplier."

"And this supplier?"

"Roof, well, he rubbed my guy the wrong way."

"And how are you rubbing your guy?"

"You know me—smooth as silk."

Hank coughed a laugh. Smooth was one of many things Blue Dog was not.

"So, the responsibility for this is not a head-scratcher?"

"Nobody scratching their heads except the po-lice."

"How can they scratch their heads same time they're scratching their balls?"

Hank had a beef with Detroit cops for turning him down just because of some juvie shit he'd pulled a long time ago. He stared at the rows of cigarettes behind Blue Dog and swore under his breath. He was wearing two nicotine patches. Big guy like him, he needed a nicotine sponge to squeeze over his fat, bald head.

Blue Dog's voice dropped, and Hank had to strain against the thick glass to hear. Hank made him repeat what he said: "There's a meet at the club tonight."

"Aw, shit," Hank said. "Shit!" He liked the sleepy-time minimum-security prison down in Toledo. And he had his big secret waiting for him in the Philippines. She called herself Missy, but he knew she had another name too, and he was going to learn how to pronounce it in person next month.

"They're finally tearing down the stadium," Blue Dog said.

"What, you trying to cheer me up? They can't tear down the stadium." Hank knew they could and would, but admitting that would be too much. Blue Dog had seen Hank's baseball card collection. Unlike other kids, Hank hadn't attached his to bicycle spokes or tossed them against cement walls. He filed them carefully in shoeboxes his grandfather gave him from J. L. Hudson's where he worked shelving stock at night.

"Sorry, Lump. I just pump gas."

Hank laughed, but the laugh tasted like it had already turned. "You haven't pumped gas in twenty years. You just sit in the box and do your fucking nails."

"Not true," Blue Dog said. He looked down at his nails rimmed with grime.

"The highest rate of suicide is for dudes who work in tollbooths. You need a hobby in there."

"Where do you get these so-called facts?"

"From the so-called newspapers."

"I already got a hobby."

"Yeah, but you can't jack off here in public. It'd scare away customers."

"Nothing scares away these customers. Guy cracked another guy with a tire iron last week. Blood all over the place."

"And . . ."

"I called 911 like a good citizen."

"Dog, you trying to get into the 'Random Acts of Kindness' column?"

"What's that?"

"It's in the newspaper, you wouldn't know. I'll see you at the meet."

"No meet for me. Conflict of interest."

"How's that work?"

"Me no speak no evil. Me no do no evil."

"You're an asshole. Fuck your bulletproof glass."

"Exactly," Blue Dog said, smiling.

"You losing more teeth?" Hank asked.

Blue Dog covered his mouth and mumbled something. Hank jangled the keys—"Thanks, my friend"—and headed back to his truck.

•••

Hank's stomach roiled with the burden of being back, all the jagged pieces roiling around, snagging. He already had a plane ticket to Manila, stashed in his inside pocket where he usually stored his smokes, against his heart. That, and the photo she sent: Sweet Missy. A Christian girl, she said. She wore a cross in the picture and nothing else. He was quitting the smokes for her.

After the Marines, he'd studied criminal justice at Wayne while working midnights at the Ford plant on Eight Mile, falling asleep in class, cramped in a tiny desk, popping speed to write his papers and stay awake at work. Popping more speed to ride with the club on weekends.

He stopped at Bray's Bellybusters, a White Castle knock-off with the same cheap, square, gray burgers, and wolfed down a half dozen while sitting at the counter watching cars and trucks zoom and rattle past on the eight lanes of Eight Mile Road, the border between Detroit and Warren, the red vein of his life. His father's last known address was visible across traffic on the Detroit side: the Bel-Air, a cheap motel/apartment building/by-the-hour locale that remained open, meeting the endless demands from the near-homeless, the horny, and the wanna-be outlaws who needed a cheap hideout.

He knew the burgers were a bad idea, but the day seemed full of bad ideas, and it was maybe the least bad of them all, and their weight might keep him from fleeing, which was the worst bad idea. No hiding out for a guy that big, that slow.

•••

Dear Missy,

I'm a big guy, but I got a big heart. Your English is fine. I will teach you more when I visit. I don't have a lot of family like you. I look forword to meeting yours.

My grandma was a singing barmaid for a time. My grandpa was a barber for a time. My ma worked as a secretary for Paramount. You might of seen some of their movies. She never met any movie stars, but sometimes she got us passes for previews of new movies and we'd take the bus downtown to see them. We liked James Bond the best. And anything with John Wayne, known as The Duke.

My mom never learned to drive. She never had money for a car. Learning to drive is important. I will teach you. I have a motorcycle, but I think it will be to big for you. I have enough money for my truck, and to feed you and our family some day.

I know this ain't the best way to fall in love, but you want some things and I want somethings and maybe there's enough things we both want so we can make it work.

I'm big, but I will not hurt you. Some people have the wrong idea because of the bike, the marines, but I am not a mean person, I am disciplined and work hard. I don't go to church. It wasn't a habit with me and my mom. I will go to church with you.

I never met the right person, and once I became a guard, they moved me around to different prisons, so I never stayed in one place until I got back to Detroit.

My Uncle Brad was my favorite. He took me to baseball games and I spent week ends with him and Aunt Suzie. Whenever I needed a ride somewhere, he drove me. He had a son that died in high school. Seeing as I didn't have a father, me and him were close. He use to give me dollar bills when I was a kid, and I bought baseball cards. I'll show them to you. It's hard to explain.

I have some guns just as a hobby, I don't shoot them around the house or nothing. And all the James Bond and John Wayne movies on video. John Wayne, people forget about him, but he was a hero in many great movies. We have so many prisons here, I'll always have work.

My friend Blue Dog's real name is Reggie, but no one calls him that. He was also writing to some body in the Philipines but he chickened out and wouldn't fly over. I won't chicken out. The Big American will be their soon. America is a great country. You won't have to get naked like that here. I will buy you lots of clothes. I have presents for all of your family, like you said.

Sincerely,

Hank

•••

He got named "Lumpy" in the club. Everyone had a club name. The president got drunk and gave them out, and "if you don't like it, lump it." You weren't supposed to challenge the president's call, but Hank didn't like his name, Mook.

"Mook," he said. "That means somebody stupid. I went to college, Brick. How about a different name?"

"Mook means somebody stupid? Hmm. If you know that, I guess you're not a Mook. Since you don't like it, your name is now Lump."

And so it was. Slightly better than Mook. Because of his size, some people assumed Hank was stupid. One of his criminal justice professors had suggested that he might be able to get into law school, but Hank had only saved enough for his bachelor's.

He parked down the block from Blue Dog's building and sat in his truck a few minutes, watching comings and goings. He trusted Blue Dog, but he didn't trust people that Blue Dog trusted—his supplier had killed one of the brothers, but Dog was trying to stay neutral. Nobody was going to tolerate that.

Some of the members led double lives, but not double lives that crossed wires so clearly as this. Hank figured Brick and the others wanted Blue Dog to set up his supplier for a hit, so Blue Dog staying home from the meet wasn't going to cut it. Dog getting lazy or careless, and his tiny fleabag apartment had no bulletproof glass to protect him, or Hank.

Hank wasn't a fan of being shot, having been wounded twice, once in Vietnam and once in Riverside. They had more similarities than one might think, he came to realize—both jungles with booby traps.

•••

Hank wanted to get cleaned up before the meet, but he'd already seen the same car drive past three times. And Blue Dog's neighborhood wasn't one you'd drive past three times unless you were lost, and, if you were lost, God help you before somebody else helped you instead.

Hank ran an already greasy comb through his thinning hair and drove over to the cinderblock clubhouse on Gratiot. Outside the club, the street clustered with cars and bikes, but as you drove past, the road emptied out and the street grid became spotted with vacant, overgrown lots—missing teeth, like Blue Dog.

•••

Dear Missy,

I bought a bigger TV so we can watch it when you come to America. It will help you learn more English. My friends in Detroit help me get discounts on things. Your so small, I don't want to buy you any cloths till you get here. I will get a special phone for you to call your family. When I said I can't believe how many brothers and sisters you have, that's just an expression. I believe you. I have not flown since I came back from Vietnam. You will like it I hope.

I don't know why we have so many prisoners in America. I just keep them in line. Drugs has a lot to do with it though. Even in prison, there's still alot of drugs. I don't do drugs. I will keep you safe.

My friend Blue Dog says I will squish you I am so big but that's not true.

•••

"Lump, man, what's the deal with your buddy, Blue Dog?"

Hank had sponsored Blue Dog when he'd been admitted into the club over ten years ago. He looked around the room at the grizzled group—only a few younger members now, guys back from Afghanistan or Iraq with sharp edges, quick triggers. Their club wasn't one of the big players in the Detroit area—nationals like Hell's Angels and Outlaws had strong local branches—but nobody laughed at the Trojan Warriors.

"My buddy?"

"Where is he?"

"At work probably."

"We think he set Roof up." The thought hadn't occurred to Hank, but things started clicking into place. Same distributor. Same merchandise. Territorial issues? Had Blue Dog taken a side? Hank hadn't been to the clubhouse in a while—living out of town, etc. Working lots of OT at Correct Corp., etc. Given his mother had died, etc. Given that she'd had so little to dispose of in Detroit, etc. Hank had bought a modest gravestone, and she was buried in Mount Olivet at Eight Mile and Outer Drive, near the abandoned Detroit City Airport, not far from the clubhouse. A quick service at the grave for her few friends and for Uncle Brad's one surviving child, the pipsqueak Billy, the last of Hank's direct relatives. He'd changed the spelling to Billie, and, to Hank, it appeared he hit from the other side of the plate now, so the family line might be screeching to a stop unless he and Missy got started.

•••

"Why don't you ask him?" Hank asked.

A spray of broken-glass laughter.

"You know Blue Dog," he continued. "He doesn't have that kind of initiative."

"He's been avoiding us in his little booth."

"How? He can't hide in there."

"We," Brick paused. Hank thought Brick had been president too long, but the club had no term limits. They looked like a parody of a motorcycle club. Mostly a bunch of flabby, balding, scraggly graybeards. "We want to make it look like a robbery, see . . ."

Hank stood, pushing himself up out of the stained, musty green couch that also needed to be replaced. It looked like it came out of someone's parents' basement years ago because in fact it had.

"You got evidence of a set up? Who's this distributor guy?"

"Some dude named Stoney. Lump, man, you ain't been around much."

"Toledo, man."

"We want the territory. We need the business. We're losing our brand."

"Your brand?"

"Our brand. You're part of it too, right?"

"I'm here, aren't I?"

"Aren't I?" One of the younger guys repeated, mocking him. It didn't take much for Hank to sweat—particularly in that stuffy little clubhouse full of old weight. He felt it beading up on his forehead and swiped it away with his forearm.

"Lump knows how to talk right. You got a problem with that?" Brick eyed the young buck—skinny guy whose cut hung on him like a Halloween costume. "He's been a noble brother who has served us well."

Hank closed his eyes for just a second to imagine Missy in a wedding dress in the sunshine of the Philippines, where he'd spent time during the war, frequenting the whorehouses designed for GIs on leave with huge hungers and heavy hearts.

"Like I said, we want this to look like a holdup. We were thinking, who could get old Blue Dog to come out of his little box for a minute, and we were thinking, Lump . . ."

Hank wanted to shake Blue Dog for being so stupid—a Mook. Thinking somehow he could sit this one out, even if he hadn't set up Roof.

"Roof was shoveling snow. How do you get a set-up out of that?"

Brick let out a gravelly sigh. "What's Toledo doing to you, my friend? He set Roof up as a target by making it look like he'd stolen merch from the distributor. Dog made him a target, whether he was shoveling snow or taking a shit. He was a marked man because Blue Dog *set him up.*"

That made sense. If it looked like a random street robbery, chances of anyone getting caught in Detroit were slim to none. If it happened in Roof's house, the cops would be at the Trojans' clubhouse in five minutes asking questions.

"What about this distributor? What's that operation?"

Brick sighed again. "I don't remember you asking so many questions, Lump."

Hank looked around at the younger guys, restless with talk. "Like you said, I've been a loyal member. Blue Dog and I go way back. I can't sell him out."

"What could get him out of the box late some night, business slow, all that?"

A truckload of porn videos? A friend on his knees with a gun to his head in the parking lot? A strung-out hooker looking for pills? In another time and another place, they'd given two hookers a jump on Christmas Eve and got rewarded while the battery was charging.

Blue Dog broke the security camera because it creeped him out. It had never been replaced or fixed.

•••

Dear Missy,

I might of gained a few pounds since that photo, but I lift weights. They have a workout room we can use when the prisoners aren't in there.

I have seen a lot of bad people in and out of prison, and I have not always been a good person, but you can count on me to take care of you. If everything works out during the visit. Where will I stay? Will we have time alone together? I live in a trailer now, but I will buy a house. It's harder to sell a trailer then I thought. If I sell it, I almost have enough for a down payment. If everything works out. I might have to sell my baseball cards—I am enclosing one so you can see what it looks like. This is one of my doubles—that means I have two of the same card. We're going to have fun explaining things to each other. My mom didn't leave me nothing accept her Christmas decorations, but she had a lot of them. She got mad when I told her I was writing you. All we had was each other for a long time. I miss her. Let's have two children, a boy and a girl.

Sure, I can bring your mother over to stay for awhile. If everything works out.

I hope this money helps your family until I get their. It must be hard to be so poor. I thought we were poor, but we always had electricity and running water.

Its important to protect myself, so sometimes I had to hurt people. I am a good man, you will see. I realized the other day that I never said I love you to anyone in my life. My mother and I didn't talk that way. James Bond never said I love you. But maybe I will say it to you someday.

Sincerely,

Hank

—The picture you sent—that's really you, right?

—Whose going to meet me at the airport? How will I recognize them?

•••

Hank had imagined he could do a fadeout as a Trojan Warrior, but because he was a wise beard now, and good with guns, and lived out of town, Brick didn't want to let him go. Hank didn't trust Brick. Or, anybody really, but particularly not Brick. A little power goes a long way on those streets. Hank had taken criminal psychology courses, laughing at the theories—they'd always been trumped by the violence in his own life. You don't have time to analyze when somebody's cracking a beer bottle over your head.

Now, everybody had guns. The rumbles with chains and tire irons, switchblades and zip guns—the quaint old days. Even in the Marines, tearing up a bar was just a thing they did, and no one died because of it.

Brick was no mastermind like James Bond and didn't have the charisma of John Wayne, yet he'd been president for fourteen years. Hank had been sergeant at arms until he moved to Toledo. Lump. He was too big to be anything else. Lump—and stuck with the last name of some white-trash loser who took a hike instead of manning up and caring for his son.

He once thought that since he'd killed in the war, maybe he could kill in club wars. Killing bad guys like John Wayne. John Wayne's real name was Marion Morrison—a sissy name, so he'd changed it. The guys in the club had newer heroes, fighters like Conor McGregor, action movie tough guys like The Rock, Vin Diesel, but he was sticking with good old John Wayne, who was also six-foot-four.

He'd done one hit for the club, and he wasn't killing anybody else—no good guys or bad guys. No more blood on the streets and driving back to Toledo like it was nothing. Up close, it turned his stomach. He knew killers in prison, and he wasn't like them. Not anymore. He was marrying a girl from the Philippines, and if she wasn't perfect, neither was he. Her own letters, short and perfumed. Direct, and he liked that. After that first one, no more naked photos. She added more layers to her story like modest clothes, pretending she'd never sent the naked one. That's how the mating service worked. What she'd signed on for, and she was honoring the deal.

•••

He thought he could walk away if he did nothing at all. Not warn Blue Dog, but not lure him out of the box. But how could he not warn Blue Dog?

"I'm not judge and jury. I'm just a prison guard."

"The young guys will handle it. Just get him out of the box and drive away."

What would John Wayne do? He'd sock somebody. What would James Bond do? He'd have some gadget to get him out of there.

"Blue Dog doesn't need to die."

"Neither did Roof."

"Just rough him up a little. He'll get the message."

"We want it to look like a robbery."

"Good luck getting him out of that box."

Hank wanted a cigarette—the room full of smoke, his throat raw with longing. Missy said she didn't smoke or drink, and why would she lie about that? Missy's last letter blurred with sweat in his back pocket.

Hank turned and walked out the heavy metal door. It slammed behind him. He stepped into the rutted street lined with motorcycles and pickups. Tomorrow, Hank would go to the viewing at Mankowski's, their funeral home of choice. To show that he was not afraid. To do what he'd come to do—pay respects.

•••

Blue Dog never came home that night. So, he knew what he knew, and Hank believed that was enough. No one spoke to Hank in Mankowski's. Keeping club business and paying respects separate was another tradition. Polite handshakes and hugs with Roof's family, though his widow was having none of it, shielding herself with family members. "Where's that bastard, Blue Bitch?" she shouted for everyone to hear.

Hank was writing down his words and sending them across the ocean. He'd show her all the old movies. He'd walk with an exaggerated John Wayne swagger. He'd tell her about baseball cards and Uncle Brad, his All-American childhood. He'd teach her how to swim.

•••

Hank drove past the old stadium on his way back to Toledo, skipping the ceremonial ride to the cemetery, veering off from the Trojan Warriors forever.

TV crews and flashing lights and cranes with wrecking balls were moving in. He hoped it would take a long time to tear it down and haul away the rubble. You didn't tear something down like that overnight. His Uncle Brad rolling over in his grave, wherever that might be. In their family, people just seemed to disappear. No one saved for a stone. Starting with his mom, everybody was getting a stone. He'd chipped in for Roof's. His wife called it blood money, but she'd taken it and asked for more.

...

Uncle Brad spent his time at the ballpark and the racetrack. The track took all his money, even money he didn't have, which was an old story, yet one that he was determined to tell. He took Hank to ballgames where they could sit in the sun and look down at the bright green, perfect grass and not lose any money. He showed Hank where to wait for autographs after the game and told him stories of the great ones—Hank Greenberg, Mickey Cochrane, Schoolboy Rowe. He knew all the players and their stats. Some of them came to the track, and they gave him tickets for his tips if he was on a lucky streak.

He once gave Hank an autographed ball signed by the whole team, a ball now stored with the old cards in Hank's trailer. Some nights when he couldn't sleep, he carefully flipped through the cards. All the guns in the world didn't help when he couldn't sleep, but the cards lulled him back into soft ballpark afternoons. He'd done shift work most of his life, but it took a long time for his body to adapt, and as soon as it did, they'd change him to another shift.

Once Uncle Brad snuck him onto the field before batting practice, and he was allowed to run the bases. Norm Cash, Hank's favorite player, a big, slugging first baseman, told his uncle, "Big boy like him, you've got to get him on a ballfield."

Riverside had no ballfield, and in the cement world of Detroit, few were available, and the kids in the projects seemed to have no interest. They needed bats, balls, and gloves, and who would be providing them? They bounced a rubber ball against the curb and tried to catch it in their hands, creating invisible base runners in a complicated system they all knew. The

bent spectacles of net-less basketball rims were all you needed to see in order
to know those kids were screwed. His mother was nearly as large as he was
until the cancer shrunk her down to nothing. His mother, who got him to
swim at the Y because it was free and she liked the idea of not drowning.

•••

When Uncle Brad started his own family with Aunt Irene, he stopped coming
around. He bought a house on the Warren side of Eight Mile and abandoned
Hank just when he was entering his teenage years as the fat white boy with
the pimply face.

Hank's mother could not replace Brad. She understood, but did not. Hank
simply did not. A couple of times, Brad picked him up on the way to a ball
game in a car loaded with his three boys. They called him Hanky and listened
to him tell stories his uncle did not approve of.

Hank had few pictures from his childhood. The last one his uncle took
was a shot of his boys in a row at Tiger Stadium beside Hank, who, due to
his size, and the distorted angle of the photo, dwarfed the others. Uncle Brad
mailed the photo to Riverside. Mail meant bills. No telling how long it sat
in their box in the long row at the front of the building before his mother
handed it to Hank one day.

•••

Hank woke up the morning of the funeral on Dog's couch. Blue Dog had
always come home. Nowhere to go besides work and the clubhouse. Hank
put his meaty fingers on the smudged keys of Blue Dog's computer and
clicked away to see if he'd left any clues, but all he found was the usual lot of
downloaded porn. The phone rang. Hank let it ring. Then, the second time,
he picked it up, thinking it might be Blue Dog. Then, whoever had called
hung up. An old trick, and Hank realized he'd fallen for it. He grabbed his bag
and headed out the door, locking it, kicking the keys underneath. He looked

down at the street. No sign of the circling car, though a cop car slowed down out front, then sped off as Hank approached his truck.

•••

He drove past the Hi-Fi. A stranger sat in the bulletproof booth. Hank slipped back onto the service drive off of Eight Mile and then onto I-75, merging into the traffic headed south, away from the funeral, toward the safety of prison. He could do nothing now to help Blue Dog. He squirted windshield washer fluid again and again to try and clear the smeared road salt. He pictured the long, angry roars of the bikes in procession, giving the appearance of logic and structure while they ran red lights because they could. He would sell his bike. His heart thudded heavy in his chest—he wasn't sure if that was good or bad. All he knew was he had a plane to catch, though even that might be one more lie. Or it might be his alibi. The Goodyear Odometer faded in the rearview mirror, stuck forever on zero. He looked down at the gas gauge. He'd forgotten to fill up. He'd have to find another station soon.

Outer Drive

. . . It starts and stops and starts again. It runs north, south, east and west, twisting in long curves and turning in sharp angles. There are residential, commercial and industrial sites, sometimes all within a few blocks of each other. . . . Outer Drive is one bizarre road, stretching more than 40 miles in a jagged horseshoe from the East Side at Mack Avenue to Jefferson Avenue in Ecorse Downriver. . . . One of the oddest city thoroughfares in the country. . . . The problem with Outer Drive is that it was built piecemeal. To expedite construction, it was linked to existing roads whenever possible.

—Curt Guyette, *Detroit Metro Times*

A police helicopter erupted in mad thuds above me, veering toward some urgent capture or rescue. I waved up at it. Just another cold, windy day on the crooked horseshoe of Outer Drive. Thanksgiving coming up. If only they were dropping turkeys from the sky.

I wore two pairs of socks on my feet and another on my hands. With enough money for a cup of coffee jingling in my pockets, I was heading out to find one. Plenty of socks, but not one damn pair of gloves. Maybe my brother, Randy, took mine.

I lived with him and his pregnant girlfriend, Emma, in our parents' old house. They were arguing in the kitchen when I came downstairs. I slunk past out them out the back door, grabbing my jacket and boots along with a fistful of socks from a random laundry basket I nearly tripped over. With the baby due in a month, my continued presence was the subject of both hushed discussion and loud debate. It didn't pay to listen, and I wasn't interested in anything that wasn't paying.

When our parents got divorced, Randy and I lived in the house with our mother, Ann, for another half-dozen years. When she moved into a small apartment with her future second husband, Gus, our father, Pat, bought the house back off her and moved in again, so we lived there with him and his future second wife, Donna. Got it? Randy was working his way through college then, and I was drinking my way through high school—we had no choice but to stay put.

Donna's entrance onto the scene had prompted the divorce—she and our father had been screwing in our family van in the parking lot of Eight Miles High, the local watering hole where ol' Pat had taken to whet his whistle most nights after second shift when we were already tucked away back home. She'd been best friends with Ann back at Eight Mile High School. An old story, I know. I wish it had a new twist. Took me and Randy a few years to get all the details—we'd be happy not to have them, even now. One rainy morning, I found my booster seat wedged tight between the back seat and the sliding van door when we climbed in for the ride to school. Strange, I thought.

Then, Donna decided she didn't want to live with our mother's furniture and decorations and rugs and stale cigarette smell (and kids)—even though she'd helped her pick out some of the stuff back in the day—so Randy bought Outer Drive off our dad after he'd tried selling it himself, asking for too much.

He saved face by selling it to Randy, who got a deal on the house in exchange for lying about what he paid for it to Donna—a decision I talked Randy into. That's how screwed up our family is—two honest guys trapped into lying. Though our father doesn't hold much to the truth anymore—hard to stop lying once you start, and when you tell whoppers, like he did to us for years, then all the others seem like small change.

I don't hate Donna anymore. Well, I still kind of do. I want to get over it, but I'm stuck there, like the needle on one of my mom's old scratchy records we danced to—me, her, and Randy—on the living room floor. The Beatles' "Twist and Shout": "work it on out / *pop* / work it on out / *pop* / work it on out." We incorporated the scratch into the dance, jumping in front of the stereo to skip the record forward over it. I need to incorporate that into my life—jump over the damage and *work it on out*.

Donna got what she deserved: my father. He isn't the prize he once was, the handsome, polite ladies' man—at least compared to some of the road scum he hung out with. She's got him dyeing his hair—though he denies it. She goes on about how he's not going gray like my uncles—despite his hair color not even matching his beard. Maybe a toupee coming up next, since he's thinning on top. Wears a ball cap when I see him now, but that's not often.

Donna always thought she was worth more, just like the house—ambitions and grudges I never figured out. I'd want her on my side in a street fight, but we've never been on the same side of anything. Our father could shave his head and tattoo his hair on, and we'd still not give a shit. She wants us to care—that want is a soft bruise on her skin, and when I see that discolored, vulnerable spot, I can't hate her.

It hollows you out, I think, that focus on looks. Or turns you a cardboard cutout anyone can knock right over. Or maybe no one even has to do it—the stench of your own bullshit blows you down.

Donna doesn't understand that we have left the arena where she is still wrestling with our mother. She thinks we're still in our seats and that Donna versus Mom is the main event. Wrestling is the right sport—no doubt about who's Good and who's Bad. I loved the certainty of it myself. When our dad took us to WrestleMania after he'd moved out and before Donna moved in, we got in a fender-bender on Outer Drive on the way home from the Silverdome. Our mother went Hulk-a-mania on him.

•••

Our dad once tried to sell used cars, but that was a bust. According to his friend Ace, who owned the lot, our dad was a mercy-fuck of a salesman—the only people who bought cars from him did so out of pity while he stumbled and fumbled and told the truth about the flaws. Our dad's not the dimmest bulb in the room, but he's not putting out a lot of watts anymore—like something's draining his will, dialing down the dimmer switch. That lack of will allowed him to spill his beers and tears to Donna at the bar till they ended up in the van. Who took who for a ride, I don't much care.

It only seems right that it's Randy's house now—we'd lived there longer than anyone. Randy knew all its flaws, and that I was one of them.

•••

Maybe our mother wouldn't have smoked so much if our dad wasn't out carousing. We watched TV with her as she filled an ashtray with one Kool after another while complaining about the price of cigarettes. We thought he was working late while he was at the bar right down the street. She worked at Eight Mile Auto Supply for years—despite the hopeless prospects for promotion or a decent raise—just so she could smoke on the job. She veers back and forth between The Patch and The Gum now, frantic with quitting, since she's going to be a grandmother soon. Not sure she's ready—to quit, or be a grandmother. The chain stores rose up and choked off the local guys, so now she's out of work. Another old story. You'd think an auto parts store could last forever in Detroit. Fuck the Pep Boys.

•••

Take Outer Drive East through Mt. Olivet Cemetery, turn left to stay on it, then it turns into State Fair at Dequindre, then disappears at Woodward only to reappear between 7 and 8 Mile Road off of Livernois as Outer Drive West . . .

I'd never been in Cubano Café, though when it'd been the Tel-Star—a dingy dive some tough guys shot up a couple years ago—I sometimes frequented the place to listen to bad local bands play loud covers. After the bloodshed, everyone fled. Boarded up for a time, now under new ownership as a café during the day and a bar at night. Maybe that's what helped them get straight with the city and the LCB—calling it a café, offering up real food, not potato chips and blind robins. Maybe they were even closing at 2 a.m. now, like they were supposed to. You could stay all night in the Tel-Star—they'd just lock the door and keep serving till dawn.

I'd never entered the place before noon, but now it was a café, and I needed my morning coffee, and maybe a donut. Wake myself up, kill time before I started making rounds on my weekly ritual of winding up and down the mile roads, stopping in at every bar and grille and hole-in-the-wall, filling out job applications whenever they were willing to hand one over.

They say bars are recession proof. They say a lot of shit, those big-time "theys" who work in skyscrapers, scraping sky—or, more accurately, the money off the sky—and catching it before it hits the ground where the rest of us are holding out our hands, wondering if it might rain, though the money-drought is a way of life and we're already rationing like they told us to.

Our parents didn't go to college, and it wasn't in my skill set to be a student. If my life is a pencil, I've been too distracted by the shavings to see the point. I was a Ritalin kid who squirmed from desk to desk, from school to school, graduating to alcohol and drugs until someone gave me a diploma to get me out of there. Home life sucked, but that's no excuse. I could've escaped, really escaped, not just hidden out in a drunken haze.

At graduation, I ran naked across the stage at Eight Mile High to wild applause. That's how I got my nickname, "Streak," now tattooed on my forearm, so every time I check my watch, I'm reminded of what an asshole I was—isn't that one of the functions of tattoos, to remind us what assholes we could be? I remember my father asking, "Why didn't you at least wear a mask?"

...

I pushed at the door, but nothing budged. I cupped my hands around the tiny square of glass and looked inside. A beefy guy, maybe an old Tel-Star veteran, nudged me aside and pulled the door open.

"Pull," he said. One of those thick steel ones. I think all bars have that same door. At least, all the ones I've been in. "Pull," he said again. Wise guy.

"It used to be Push," I said. Maybe since I'd quit drinking, my wires got reversed.

"Got to change with the times," he said, and tipped his greasy mesh ball hat in my direction. I ceremoniously held the door open as he entered, then slipped in behind him.

A steel door didn't keep Sophie, the Tel-Star owner, from getting killed in a robbery. Her son, Bart, tried to keep the place going, but those were the cocaine-cowboy days, and Bart wasn't so good at keeping his nose clean and his hands out of the till without his mother there to slap them away. Six months later, the wild-west, drug-turf shootout dimmed the stars for good.

•••

Donna hadn't broken up our family, but she'd created the first crack—like a pebble dropped from the truck in front of you on the freeway that bounces up and pocks your windshield, and that spreads into a crack that road vibrations slowly push into a jagged dividing line.

Donna and our mom hated each other. Our mom has her faults—she still brings up blowjobs in the van all these years later while Randy and I exchange pained looks. But she always put us first, and the three of us are hardwired together. Randy and I had to be tight to get through the moving in and moving out and who got invited to our birthday parties and who was drinking too much and who was selling cocaine and who was getting fired.

Randy hadn't said anything directly to me yet about being the grinding third wheel, but if I was going to be a father (yeah, right), I wouldn't want anybody else—even my cool-cat brother—slurping Cheerios at the table every morning while I staggered sleepless through the house looking for a clean diaper.

•••

I was twenty-five, with no career path. No career back alley. I mocked the word "career" as some kind of inside joke with myself. After Eight Mile, I'd spent all of a half semester at Macomb Community College, known affectionately as Twelve Mile High—not real college, I wasn't good enough. I'm no smartass like Randy, but I wasn't such a dumbass to not know at least that much. Randy paid his own way through Wayne State. No one in our family had gone before. Ace, one of my godfathers, had gone. That's how fucked up we were—I have two godfathers, which no one has properly explained to me. We never even went to church, so how did I get two godfathers?

I scraped bottom when I traded my car—a Plymouth Satellite with an engine I'd rebuilt myself—for cocaine, and not a lot of it. After that, I had no job, and no way to find or get to a job. Randy stepped up and muscled me into rehab. He might still be paying off that bill—I'm afraid to ask.

My dad asked how many grams I got for it. My mother slapped me in the face, said I made her sick, told me to get out.

I lost some weight in rehab. Pulled myself together enough to think I could leave town and made the bold move to Pennsylvania to work on a fracking site with my Uncle Stan, my dad's brother. That lasted all of three months. Draw your own conclusions with thick crayons on construction paper.

•••

. . . then crosses the Lodge and Southfield freeways, then turns left past the community college across W. McNichols, also known as 6 Mile Road across Grand River . . .

Back on Outer Drive, I got a job at the Fuel & Fuddle as a grill cook and all-around cleanup guy. Two years of a steady life, then they ran out of fuel to keep the lights on. I never wondered what Fuddle meant, but I got time on my hands, so I looked it up in the library, one of my current hangouts. It means "drunk," or "to get somebody drunk." I assumed it was some Irish or Scottish thing, since that was the theme of the place, designed to resemble a pub. Or an American TV version of a pub, which was the only version I knew, so I thought it looked authentic. Guinness on tap. And being a Callahan, shouldn't I fit right in?

•••

"Should I get married?" Randy asked.

"Not if it means I have to move out," I said.

"Fuck you," he said. "I'm serious—is it the right thing to do?"

"I'm not exactly a fountain of wisdom on these things." I was looking at my beat-up sneakers, wondering why I used to care how clean they were.

"A fountain of wisdom? Where you come up with this shit? Brother, you gotta find a job that takes advantage of your way with words."

"Just don't get all wishy-washy like dad," I said, "In fact, don't ask Dad. If you decide to get married, just don't invite him and the Best Friend."

After a long pause, he cleared his throat and said, "You gotta move out. Like, yesterday."

•••

Randy was four years older. Our parents got married as soon as my mom got pregnant—no indecision back then. Grandpa Turner had more than one shotgun. They had Randy, then me, then ol' Pat got his vasectomy and really started fooling around.

"We were too young, we didn't know what we were doing," our parents say. But we were too young too—Randy and me—to witness all that. Our job was to be nice to everyone:

"Be nice to Donna."

"Be nice to Gus."

"Did you tell her it was a great meal?"

"Did you thank him for taking you fishing?"

As kids, we didn't know what being nice meant. Not hit them? Share our toys with them? It was our job, but nobody was paying us in any recognizable currency.

•••

We ended up with four sets of grandparents, and our holidays became a leaky barrel of forced laughs.

We barely had one grandparent now. Three were dead, four hardly acknowledged us as grandkids (too old when we joined their families), while the one who loved us, our father's mother, the one we called "Plain Grandma," was dying in her tiny house in River Rouge.

"Why don't we invite Plain Grandma to live with us?" I asked Randy.

"You gonna share your room with her, Vinnie?"

I shrugged. A charity case myself, I had overstepped. I stepped back.

"Anyone invite us for Thanksgiving? Who can we piss off this year?" Randy and I stood in the kitchen. He was drinking a beer after work, and I was keeping him company while Emma was at her breastfeeding class at Mercy. The ancient radio we'd garbage-picked when we were kids was blaring some oldies station—the clock was busted, but we couldn't even tell time back then. It was one thing that nobody had given us or made us feel guilty about. If I had to move out, I was taking it with me.

"Emma's ma asked us. We'll be gone all day. Sorry, brother, you're on your own." He put his hand on my shoulder like he always did, measuring me or holding me back.

"I'll stay here and watch the Lions lose," I said. "Don't worry about little old Vince. Guess you guys need a break from me."

Randy started to say something, then stopped. "We'll bring you a piece of pie," he said.

"Pumpkin, a big piece," I said. "And apple too, if they have it—a little combo for your favorite brother."

"Beggars can be losers," Randy said.

"Choosers—it's 'can't' and 'choosers.' 'Beggars can be losers.' I don't even understand that."

"We're going to have to stop cussing when the baby comes."

"Yeah, you're going to have to shut the fuck up." I meant it as a joke, but it came out sharp.

"Emma will kill both of us, brother, if you don't get out. I mean it."

"She'll kill me first."

"Well, that goes without saying," he said, and punched my arm. ·

"Maybe I'll go talk turkey with Plain Grandma," I said. "We'll commiserate over cold mashed potatoes from the Colonel."

"Give her this." He pulled out some folded bills and handed them over. I made a show of grabbing an envelope from the closet and stuffing the cash in. It'd been a long time since he'd trusted me with money, so I didn't want to spoil the moment.

Donna had grudged big time against Plain Grandma for not welcoming her with open arms, so our grandmother moving in with them was not on their plate, table, in their house, or remotely in their vicinity. Shit, Grandma didn't have no open arms—she was busy holding onto her walker. Randy and I loved her, and we loved my mother, and our grandmother and mother loved each other like mother and daughter, though they could not see each other now except on occasions that involved us, the grandkids—public gatherings where they spoke briefly and in code while Randy and I kept our mother and Donna from popping all the balloons of civility. Every family get-together became a dust-up, with pregame strategies and audibles at the line of scrimmage. Big-time, post-game analysis. Our grandmother had recently been scolded for sitting at the same table as our mother at Emma's baby shower. She didn't have the strength anymore.

•••

I was kicking in part of my unemployment check to Randy for utilities and food. I still needed my pickup, so insurance, gas, and upkeep put another dent in my nearly totaled budget. In Detroit, if you don't have a car, you're screwed—public transport was blasphemy in the Motor City. The pickup was the one Grandpa Pete had his heart attack in, though somehow he carefully pulled over onto the shoulder and put his emergency flashers on to die. Grandpa Pete, our dad's dad, never wanted to be a bother to anyone, even while dying.

With almost everybody out of work, a lot of folks drove without insurance, since the rates were so high. High because so many people drove without insurance—one of the many Detroit Catch-22s. It was more like Catch-222. Detroit is laid out in a series of grids, but that doesn't mean we don't end up driving in circles—even misshapen circles like Outer Drive.

•••

... across Grand River where you turn right onto Outer Drive W in front of Stoepel Road Park past Evergreen to Lasher Road where you turn left to stay on Outer Drive W then go under I-96 ...

"You love her?"

"You know I do," Randy said. He'd said it before, but I asked again, skeptical, never having uttered those words myself. My one serious girlfriend was a Chaldean from Eight Mile High, Amena Abbos.

My father, Mr. Gullible, bought a painting off the side of the road and hung it on his basement wall—firefighters shooting Saddam Hussein down off the flaming World Trade Center like he's King Kong. *The Chaldeans are Christians*, I told him a thousand times. He thinks those weapons are still buried out in the sand somewhere. Mass Destruction. We're all unexploded bombs, and the jury's out on whether we're all duds or just waiting for proper ignition.

Thus, my family did not approve, and thus, Amena's family did not approve of my family not approving. But we hung on for half our senior year before Amena herself did not approve. I was hoping to at least make it to the prom, but I got time off for bad behavior. Like everything else, I'm still not over her.

•••

Randy made decent money as a loan officer at the Belmont branch of NBD—National Bank of Detroit—using his accounting degree from Wayne to keep himself out of the factory when the factory was still an option. I gave him a toy badge when he got the job and started calling him Officer Callahan. I couldn't let the joke die, despite his obvious irritation. I held on to any joke I could, their frayed ropes running through my hands, burning off skin, but still I held on. Our great-uncle Joe Callahan had been a lieutenant in the Detroit Police force until he turned the gun on himself. None of us were officer material.

•••

With the due date approaching, everyone was freaking out. The first grandchild. The first of a lot of things. I tried to stay away and let Randy and Emma have time together. Emma told me that'd be a good idea in her sweet way that always got me gulping and nodding assent. Nowhere to hide in that house, even in my room, the one Randy and I had shared as kids. They shared our parents' old room, and just like back then, I didn't want to hear any sex coming out of it. I still had earplugs from my brief stint at the Ford plant, and I wedged them in tight every night. I couldn't get my own place until I got a decent job.

•••

At the public library, Dorothy Bush Branch—everything was a branch, but there was no trunk, or, the tree of Detroit was rotting, branches held on with duct tape and mirrors—I hung out among the homeless. I suppose I fit right in—scruffy beard, socks for mittens, ostentatiously rattling newspapers, secretly napping in the grimy orange chairs. I do know how to use a computer, and that's where I'd check the want ads. I made a big deal of signing up for computer time and getting online, opening up my small spiral notebook to jot down phone numbers and addresses. I have an email address. I have a password. I winked at the homeless guys to try to make myself feel superior.

To be honest, I felt shame—but why should anyone be ashamed to be in a library, one of the safest places on earth?

•••

Cubano Café. I've been stalling—my metaphorical coffee getting cold.

Why they thought of giving the place a Mexican name in the heart of our angry white neighborhood was beyond me. But then, a lot of things were—like not understanding the language was Spanish not Mexican, and the country was Cuba, not Mexico. They'd given the place this weird makeover. The walls now featured large, garish paintings of rock stars. Bowie, Dylan, Lennon, Marley, Madonna, Seger. Some, I couldn't tell—Springsteen in a headband, or a young Willie Nelson? Jagger, or Steven Tyler? Prince, or Little Richard? It no longer had the Tel-Star's sour smell: stale beer and industrial-strength cleanser layered beneath the haze of last night's cigarette smoke.

Three midnight-shifters from the Ford plant where I'd once worked sat sprawled at a table near the door draining a pitcher of beer, and the genius door-guru joined them. I didn't like drinking alone, but coffee was differ-ent—coffee was my friend. The steam. The heat. The hands around the cup.

"Nice gloves," the woman behind the bar said.

"Sock puppets," I said, giving her a sheepish smile. I opened and closed their mouths as if to make them speak, but they remained silent. She was young and cute—in the Tel-Star, she would've needed a police escort just to get from the bar to the door.

"Coffee," I said. "Please."

They had two insulated pitchers. You push the button on top and coffee squirts into your cup: regular and decaf. If they were serious about being a café, they'd have to get a big machine to cranked out the noise and steam—coffee came with a sound-and-smell show at most places now.

She filled my cup and laid a saucer on the bar—maybe they called it a counter now—along with a dish of plastic creamers and a box of sugar packets.

The Tel-Star was in the neighborhood, and I'd appreciated the option of walking home, particularly after getting a DUI one night, caught drifting recklessly down one of the nice parts of Outer Drive, the red flashers strobing silently off stately brick colonials.

I swiveled my seat around and took in the gallery. "Just like the Rock and Roll Hall of Fame," I said.

"Yeah, just like it," she said, smiling. The TV aired NBA highlights with the sound off.

Then I noticed another painting propped against the wide mirror behind the bar. A female nude. Her tattooed arms covered her breasts, but her shaved pussy was brazenly displayed. I looked again at the woman behind the bar. Long blonde hair? Check. Nice body? Check. High cheekbones? Check. Long sleeves, so I couldn't tell about tattoos.

I dumped in two sugar packets after giving the coffee a taste. I wasn't fussy about coffee as long as I could sweeten it up. I didn't use those fake creamers anymore though. Somebody told me that the stuff never got digested, that it stayed inside you forever, a sour white swamp mucking things up when you got old.

•••

They'd replaced glass block with real windows to let light in, or maybe so people could see that it was safe to go inside.

The Old Vince would have said something to her about the painting. Was I still Old Vinnie? I was going to be an uncle soon, and that was blowing my mind a little. *Fuckin' A, I'm gonna be an uncle*, I wanted to tell somebody. Maybe this sweet young lady. I stirred in the sugar, flinching at a hacking cough from one of the old-timers. He looked over at me and shook his head in some odd noncommittal way. Behind the bar, back through the open window to the kitchen, a young Black guy scraped his spatula against the grill, frying up bacon and eggs.

...

Why did I still have it in for Donna? I was old enough to know how casual betrayals shadow our lives, and how mad lust erupts out of nowhere and seems to offer no choice but to dive in. Hell, I'd felt it for Emma some days when we were alone in the house together. Her dark hair, thin frame, fierce eyes that drove me outside to wander cold, brooding streets. Emma had a primal quality—a chemical she gave off or something—which Randy had responded to. He met her when he was just a kid, didn't see her for years, then he runs into her at some club, and boom, they're in mad love all over again. I was not immune from feeling her pull. It shamed me, but I felt it.

A spike plunged through me when I looked at the painting and back at the woman. It embarrassed and aroused me—mostly aroused. It had to be her. It was her, right? If Randy was with me, like in the old days, I'd have asked for confirmation. That's what Randy and I gave each other, confirmation: Yes, you love Emma. Yes, that's definitely her. And the unspoken: No matter what, I would never try to make a move on Emma.

"Do you guys have any, like, donuts?" I asked. Yeah, I was a real smoothie with the ladies.

"We have muffins," she said. "Fresh baked." If I asked who the artist was, would that seem like a come on?

"Are muffins really healthier than donuts?" I asked. Everyone had muffins now, but weren't they just as full of calories and sugar?

"We like to pretend they are," she said, leaning toward me, her head resting on elbows akimbo against the bar.

I wanted to ask who *we* was. After years of trying to hit on any woman who was remotely kind, years of taking everything deliberately the wrong way—*I'd like to get myself some of that freshly baked, know what I mean, honey?*—I was superstitiously and religiously trying to make up for it by being polite and under control. I hadn't had any sex for, like, forever. Some level of discourse existed that contained flirting but wasn't crude—something in between, and I was missing it. Randy had found it with Emma. Going to college had civilized him in some basic way I had yet to learn.

"Do you call this a counter now, or is it still a bar?" I asked.

"You from the Tel-Star days? You don't look that old."

"Sophie served everybody." I shrugged. "My brother and I used to come here." I almost told her we grew up just around the corner, but I didn't want to unwrap the messy package of our childhood, confide in the bartender like they always did on TV.

"I'll take a muffin," I said. "Blueberry?"

"Coming right up," she said, with the cheerfulness of a game-show host or weather forecaster, a little too sincere and enthusiastic. Almost desperate—maybe trying to scare away Sophie's stubborn ghosts. She took it out of the display rack behind her with plastic tongs and put it on a plate, then took my coffee cup. *Squirt, squirt, squirt*, she filled it again. Her short, tight shirt pulled up above her wrist, and I glimpsed a tattoo. How old was she? She looked like half local TV anchor, half topless dancer.

I took a sip, added more sugar. "Better than the burned stuff they used to have."

"Tel-Star had coffee?"

"You know," I said, not sure she did, "Bars always have a pot sitting on a coil getting fried. Anyone drunk enough to order coffee can't tell the difference."

The cook handed her a plate of bacon, eggs, and toast, and she took it over to the factory rats. He wiped his hands on a clean rag and sighed, looking out over the nearly empty café.

•••

. . . and do a zig and a zag through River Rouge Park and across Warren and Ford Roads (if you hit Telegraph you've gone too far) across Michigan Avenue (you're in Dearborn now, by the way) . . .

I'd put in a few months at Ford's before the big downturn. I hated the monotony but had just started resigning myself to doing my time when I got laid off. The golden handcuffs removed, and I was free to do what?

Factory jobs were long gone now, unless you were the age of the old farts at the table or knew somebody who knew somebody—all my father knew was his wife's best friend, and all she knew was how to fuck in a truck. I know—cheap shot, grow up, all that, but I'm saying it anyway. It's that nondairy creamer stuck in my gut from all the times I didn't know better.

Gus got me in at Ford's. Gus—retired now. He'd put in his thirty, and they gave him a little extra moolah to hit the road. Gus might be out deer hunting with his real sons right now. He had interfered as much as anyone, always comparing me to his boys, and to Randy, taking my mother's side in battles we'd already fought—family arguments we were used to having and didn't take seriously. We never called him dad, and he never asked.

•••

The dry muffin disintegrated in my hand, and crumbs fell to the counter. The cook swung through the kitchen's wooden half-door to the narrow space behind the bar. "Hey," he said, and I nodded. He gave the woman a peck on the cheek as he passed. She hummed. Glad I'd kept my mouth shut. I brushed my crumbs into a pile and scooped them onto a thin, useless napkin—at least it wasn't covered with bad jokes, like the Tel-Star's. I swiveled around to watch cars pass on Outer Drive through those bright new windows. By the door, the men ate and drank. Quiet, but not the nervous quiet of the sedated library, where they had signs to shush you.

The ancient jukebox, polished up and plugged in, gave off a faint glow. New life for the relic as part of the music theme. A small, square wooden platform sat in a distant corner—I think it was a dance floor at one time, or storage for empty beer cases, or room for a couple of extra tables during the good days. Now, an upright piano sat on it. Guitar case, mike stand.

I imagined performing one of my originals—I'd played guitar since high school—getting offered a job, having Kid Rock (who I had actually met one night at a party, a total asshole, but never mind)—Eminem, Bob Seger, somebody comes in and hears me. I get a record contract, go on to fame and fortune, just like in the movie pictures of my imagination. And my dad, who was in a band in high school called the Carburetors, and Donna, they want to see one of my shows but can't get tickets—do I give them a pair, let bygones *be* gone?

I only played now when Randy and Emma were both out, which these days was rarely. The house had always been too small. For fifteen years, we'd shared a bunk bed in the room I now slept in. I used to listen to Randy breathe. Now, Emma did. That house had seen a lot of crumbling, but it was still standing.

•••

"Do you have any openings?" The woman's name was Sandee—with two e's, no y, she said. She stepped in front of the painting, and I doubted my certainty—my certainty about everything—it didn't take much, given the tenuous state of daily life. "For help? You know, work."

Up close, she had the slightly haggard beauty common in the old neighborhood. Dyed blonde, thick mascara. Wariness even in her bright smile.

"We're just getting started," Sandee said. "You have any experience?"

"That I do," I said. "Cooked at Fuel & Fuddle for two years till they went under." I took my loose change from the counter and jiggled it in my hands. "I could fix everything on your menu, tend bar too." I straightened my shoulders. "I could bounce out the bad guys."

She laughed and glanced behind me. "I'm afraid nobody needs bouncing around here. Leave me your name and number." She pushed a pad and a chewed-up pencil toward me.

What she didn't say was that times were tough, since she knew that I knew that everybody knew. I stacked my coins on the counter. The factory guys called out for another pitcher. Sandee filled one up and brought it over. Bud and Bud Light on tap. Which was Cubano?

The factory guys were killing time, as if the hours in the bar were part of their shift. They'd go home and sleep just long enough to allow themselves time to get up and go in again at midnight. In other words, the lucky ones with steady work.

...

"Why don't you guys like Donna?" Emma asked.

"C'mon," I said. "I'm sure Randy told you the whole story."

"Yeah, but my dad screwed around too and my parents got divorced and nobody hates each other."

"I'm waiting for you to say 'anymore.'"

"Okay, 'anymore.' But it didn't take forever. Donna was young and stupid—she doesn't have a monopoly on that."

Emma seemed to want some concession. "Okay, if it hadn't been Donna, it would've been someone else," I said. "But why'd my dad have to pick someone with such a chip on her shoulder about everything?"

"She doesn't have a chip."

"You can't see it because her big hair covers it up."

"If I wasn't eight months pregnant, I'd get up and give you a sock," she said.

"Give me a sock?" I said, jumping back from the couch where she sat sprawled. We both laughed.

I patted my shirt pocket and took out a pack of cigarettes. "Going out for a smoke," I said. "You're cute when you get mad," I added. Then, "Being pregnant makes you even more beautiful," I said, and that was true.

"Fuck you. I bet you say that to all the girls," she shot back.

"I'm still young and stupid," I said.

"Young and stupid . . . That includes me and your brother," she said. "I'm sure he's told you *that* story."

"You mean about how getting you pregnant was some version of the immaculate conception and he was an angel impregnating you?"

She coughed a hard laugh. I put the pack of cigarettes back in my pocket.

"In my version, I'm the angel," she said.

"In all my versions, I'm the angel too," I said, sitting back down. "I put that on my resume, but nobody's hiring angels these days."

"Go back to school, you asshole," she said. "It's not too late. Look at me." Emma was three classes away from a civil engineering degree at Wayne State.

"As you know, my folks never quite got the whole college fund going."

"Your grandpa left you that Ford stock."

The stock Randy used to pay for college at Wayne State—that, and two part-time jobs.

"That stock is sitting parked out front," I said.

"Your grandfather gave you that. That stock went up your nose," she said. I stood at the window staring at the truck, imagining Grandpa Pete sitting behind the wheel, engine idling, waiting for me.

"I'm learning to build bridges, Vinnie. You've got to stop burning them down," she said.

"I think I'll have that cigarette now," I said, fake creamer curdling inside me yet again and forever.

•••

The Black guy came back around and introduced himself as Ricardo. He led me behind the bar into the kitchen and asked me to make a Bloody Mary and an omelet. Sandee drank the Bloody Mary and ate the omelet at a table by the jukebox while Ricardo and I talked. She gave us both two thumbs up when she finished.

"I did the paintings . . ." he said, stretching his arms out as if to embrace them all. I was staring at the nude. "That's not Sandee," he said, jerking his head toward her.

"You mean—she looks—"

"It's my imagined idea of what she would look like," he explained, his palms turned upward on the bar in front of him as if praising a miracle. "I did it before we even met. I used to do tattoos over on Van Dyke—painting while waiting for customers. One day she walks in. She doesn't have the same tattoos," he gestured at the portrait, "but I got so freaked out, I showed her the painting. The rest . . . is history."

I wanted to ask what tattoos he'd given her, but I was a little freaked out myself for another reason: I pushed up my sleeve to show him the dragon that spewed fire across my shoulder.

"When did I do that?" he asked.

"Year before last, best I remember."

"You're hired, by the way," he said. "You'll be working weekend nights till closing. Come in Friday at four."

"Thanks. A lot." I nearly shouted. I didn't even ask about pay.

"I did a lot of dragons," he said.

"I suppose I could've come up with something more original."

"That's why I liked doing them—the challenge of making my own work distinct. That's a fine-looking dragon," he said, "but who did that shit?" He gestured to the "Streak" tattoo.

I must've given him a stricken look because he clasped my arm. "Don't worry about it, *Streak*. It'll be nice having somebody from the neighborhood working here . . . Not a lot of brothers this side of Eight. Hiring a nice white boy like you might help take the edge off a little . . . You get inspired, let me know, and I'll hook you up with some more ink. Only benefit that comes with the job, I'm afraid."

I had gotten a job and knew I should leave before he took it back. I could skip the library. I stood up from the barstool and wavered, briefly lightheaded.

"And then," he said, flourishing with his hands yet again, "I dreamed I opened a café bar. Let's hope my luck holds."

"Hope it rubs off on me," I said. "Maybe I'll start painting up some dreams myself."

"I wish you the best with that, my friend," he said.

Back at the house, Emma might be taking a nap. Randy, at the bank, loaning money to people who had none. Everyone was wishing for the best.

Ricardo gave me a genuine smile, and Sandee grinned at us both as she came back to the bar with her empty plate. I smiled too—smiles all around. Maybe it was my lot in life to be a third wheel. I was happier than I should have been, but I just let that sunshine wash over me, knowing, as we know in Detroit, that all sunshine is temporary.

"I play a little too," I said, motioning to the stage.

"Yeah, we all do," he said, laughing, "Now get out of here."

I walked toward the door in near silence, my footsteps heavy against the floor, pausing at the jukebox to look over the selections, many of them written in by hand—I imagined those old records had earned their scratches. I nodded to Mick/Steven as I headed past the wall of fame. I remembered to push—not pull—my way out.

•••

... then do a dogleg to the right across I-94 and 75 all the way to Jefferson downtown (Detroit) out past Zug Island (Don't turn right or you'll end up on the Ambassador Bridge to Canada.) and if you stay on Jefferson long enough . . .

I like saying I lived on Outer Drive, since that could mean just about anywhere around Detroit—hard for people to label you—no one knew where the hell you lived. It could be a mansion, or a dump. Vague, yet specific. Living on Detroit's oddest road, we were hidden in plain sight. All our family dramas had plenty of room to roam across the Detroit grid, drift and fade. We made jokes like "we have no inner drive on Outer Drive." We were like ordinary people in a communist country—nothing made sense, everything corrupt, and in lieu of cheap vodka, cynicism was the best medicine. Randy and I, we'd had enough half-baked apologies and raw hatred.

We used to get in a car and drive just to get out of the house, back when we were living with Donna and gas was cheaper. "Hey, here's our street," Randy'd say, and we'd be thirty miles from home in a neighborhood we'd never seen before. Outer Drive, an imaginary ring road designed to get you lost—to lose time, not save it. We'd stumble onto it in the most unlikely places.

•••

Randy ran into Emma the second time around at Eight Miles High. I know from experience that a drinking establishment can be the worst place to meet someone—to fall in love, or just pretend—but fall they did. Perhaps their old puppy love served as an antidote to the venom of loneliness and booze.

They'd first met at a campground while we were on the only vacation of our twisted childhood. In a desperate attempt to briefly weasel back into marriage, my father had borrowed Grandpa Pete's musty old house tent and put down stakes at a little family-run campground on the shores of Tea Lake, one of Michigan's many inland bodies of water generously labeled "lake." That week, it was endowed with an unfortunate algae bloom. To counteract that, Randy and Emma bloomed into each other's arms.

•••

All Randy could say was, "I used a rubber." All Emma could say was—despite being an only child—"Women in our family are very fertile."

"You crazy kids," I laughed, but my heart thudded fast and thick when they told me she was pregnant.

•••

You might not think walking in an odd place like Cubano would make much difference in a man's life. A man looking for work and maybe a little scrap of future he could hold onto until he found another scrap to glue to it. Cubano, the kind of joint you knew wouldn't make it: bad location, bad shootout-juju, and a menu and theme nobody would figure out until they were already closed for six months.

Randy and I used to make bets on how long new joints would last as they opened and closed around us. The Fuel & Fuddle made a nice go of it for a few years with the Irish thing—until the recession thing. Some people dream of opening a restaurant or bar or coffee shop, not understanding they'll lose money for years just trying to get it going. I could tell Ricardo and Sandee, as nice as they were, didn't have that money to lose—though just inhabiting their dream for a lazy morning softened me up, blurred the future's harsh edges I knew were coming. *Nice* don't pay the bills, my dad's ex-friend Ace used to say. I'd go along for the ride for a while. Maybe get a free tattoo. No more dragons. I've been thinking maybe an arrow on my spine and the words *this way up*.

...

Living with Randy had been my anchor. He kept me from slipping away like a lot of guys from Eight Mile who turned into angry young men who bought guns and drugs out of car trunks and off streetcorners and laid claim to their piece of the underside of the pie.

That old house, despite its shrunken heart, was still my lifeline. And if Randy was going down with the ship, I wanted to be on it, not doing the doggie paddle toward an imaginary lifeboat. Would either parent take me back in? I sunk into a deep funk just thinking about it.

My father wasn't talking to me. I hadn't apologized to Donna for siding with their neighbor in a dispute about his tree hanging over their yard. They'd had me over for a peace-pipe cookout, and things got out of hand. . . . Long story. Always a long story. And, yeah, it's on me too.

The whole muddy history we can't agree on enough to slog our way forward: who slept with who first and how that all went down, who took care of us and who didn't—and with a grandkid coming down the pike, it'd mean more occasions for our parents and their pardners to deal with each other—all those sweet family get-togethers soured by lingering blame—in order to share the same space with a grandchild blissfully ignorant, as opposed to everyone else's willed ignorance.

I knew my role: uncle. Where I was going to live was another question—my little piece of shit to carry around as the clock ticked down, inconvenient as hell, and mostly unspoken.

...

My mom and Gus lived out in the country near Monroe. Gus—retired, sober, regular churchgoer. My mom—still hooked on cigarettes, standing out on the porch, crying and smoking, looking out into the dark edge of nothing on which they lived. Yeah, crying. I've stood smoking there with her, and I might be doing so again soon.

Comparisons to Gus's own sons, who owned three Dairy Queens together (the Dairy Queen Kings), unspoken also. The Kings hadn't offered me a job, and I didn't expect them to, given the economy, given all the stone-cold shoulders we'd given each other from day one. Besides, I didn't want a step-job from my stepbrothers to mess up the good side of things with my mother, to be part of a debt she owed. She'd earned the right not to get infected yet again by family and money.

...

Thanksgiving morning, I lay in bed listening to Emma and Randy taking turns in the bathroom. They were out of the house by ten. The Lions game started at noon, and watching them lose would keep one tradition alive.

Unlike right after the divorce, when my mom and dad fought over where we spent holidays, we were on our own now. I was a pawn with no strategic value. No more prizes or revenge to be gained, or maybe they were resting up for battles over grandkids. Their unemployed, uneducated son could fend for himself, right?

I stewed in self-pity through the typical Lions loss, then I felt the residual hunger-memory of the after-game feasts. Few places are open on Thanksgiving, an obvious fact that sank in quickly as I dropped down onto I-75 at Eight Mile and headed away from the city. Restaurants off the interstates were usually open, and I found myself at a rusty link in a burger chain that I don't feel up to naming. Just pick one.

I was surprised by the crowd—families with little kids coming home from grandma and grandpa's, still hungry for toys in their happy meals.

Back when our father had us on weekends, we often ended up in a place like that—he couldn't cook and didn't have money to take us anywhere else. We'd play in the McFunland or whatever they called it (okay, it was McDonald's)—their big germ pit full of balls, the pissy-smelling slide. Randy and I spent hours in there, even when we were too old, just to avoid listening to our father tell us about how great Donna was and how he couldn't wait for us to meet her. Or, after we met her, *isn't she great*?

Until the time Randy finally had enough and raised a finger bloody with ketchup to point at him. "So, tell us, Dad, what's a blowjob?"

•••

. . . you'll end up in tony old Grosse Pointe Park where if you turn left at some point and head over to Mack and turn right you'll hit Outer Drive E again at Chandler Park. You are now running parallel to I-94 . . .

"You really gotta move out," Randy said. "You know, right?"

We stood on the front stoop smoking.

"You'll have to quit smoking," I said. "You know, right?"

"It was fine before, but, man, I'm freaking out. I'm gonna be a dad, and I need room to freak out."

"My unemployment check not good enough for you?"

"Mom said you could move in with them."

"Oh, so you're handling it all? You—you talked to her about this? Behind my back?" He'd taken the step I needed to but hadn't.

"Brother," he sighed, "You're not all I got anymore."

I stormed into the house, then stomped up to my room and slammed the door like a bratty kid.

•••

After my Not-So-Happy Meal, I picked up some McNuggets to take by Grandma's—she too, alone on Thanksgiving. I stopped by her grimy house in River Rouge under the I-75 overpass. The house stank of old people, old dog, and a general lack of cleanliness. She, who had put such stock in cleanliness, had finally given up, with only cable TV and her dog for company. Old Sarge was on his last legs, and so was she. Two years ago, she said she'd move out when the dog died. I sat down and patted Sarge's chest and held my hand there to feel if he was breathing. After her last serious fall, we briefly ran around looking into assisted living facilities—she claimed Sarge had saved her life, but it wasn't clear how (in fact, she might have tripped over him)—but we'd let it slide. No one was pushing Grandma out, that much was clear.

Plain Grandma dug into her nuggets and fries. Meals on Wheels had brought her a turkey dinner the day before, but she and Sarge had polished that off long ago. She still had her appetite.

"Your father called this morning," she said, and rolled her eyes dramatically. "It sounded like he was whispering from the closet so she-who-must-not-be-named wouldn't hear."

She and I shared a dislike of Donna—I tried not to get her going, since the whole thing depressed her. She didn't have much to think about, so she gnawed the bones of our family grudges.

"Emma's looking real pregnant," I said. "You ready to be a great-grandma? I mean, you're already a *great* grandma . . ."

My goal on every visit was to get a smile out of her, and I got one then.

•••

I stepped outside into the reassuring stench of River Rouge—it meant people were working, even on the holiday. The river was polluted, but not rouge. Rouge—that was the gaudy makeup of our grandmother's cheeks that she still applied religiously, if only to sit in her house all day.

•••

When you're driving up from the south on I-75, the Rouge overpass offers the first glittering glimpse of Detroit in the distance, even while the combined stench from the refinery and steel mill blasts its way through your closed windows. As I drove north, the mirage of downtown lights began to hum its quiet glow, offering up measured hopefulness as long as I didn't inhale.

Thanksgiving had been the day each year that Detroit showed its face to the nation—first the Hudson's parade, then the football game. Fuck Macy's lip-synced made-for-TV balloon spectacle. In your face, New York. For many years, the only football game was in Detroit. Then, TV took over—they're up to three Thanksgiving games now. Or is it four?

When we were kids, our parents took us to the parade. My dad brought a ladder, and we sat on its steps so we could see above the tall people. My mom packed a thermos of hot chocolate. Just another happy family in Detroit, celebrating being together, waiting for Santa to arrive on the final float, then heading home for the football game, then turkey. Walking back to the car, we held hands like we never did the rest of the year. In fact, forget the handholding—we never even walked anywhere else together.

I can't help thinking, if only my father could have carried that ladder everywhere to look over the tall people, to see what was coming in the distance, maybe he could have caught some of those turkeys falling from the sky.

•••

I drove by Cubano on my way back from Plain Grandma's, though I knew it was closed. I imagined Ricardo and Sandee sitting in somebody's house where they'd all come to terms with an interracial marriage—something more substantial, ultimately, than the pedestrian somebody-fucking-somebody-else that we were stuck with.

El Cubano is what Sandee's family called Ricardo. The world was one big inside joke, and if I was going to get any laughs out of life, I'd better get in on it. Not like I'm going to go out and paint a picture of a beautiful woman and have her walk in the door, but maybe there's another tattoo out there with my name on it.

•••

After leaving Cubano Café the day I got the job, I spent the rest of the afternoon in the pregnancy and mothering section of the library. When I got back to the house, Emma sat sprawled on the couch in the living room, waiting to talk.

"I can't let you stay," she said, struggling to lift herself into a sitting position. She had only gained weight in her belly—everything else was just as thin, or thinner.

"Yeah, my mom told me I could crash with them for a while."

"Really?"

I laughed—it hurt a little, but I did. "They got room for me. Hey, I got a job—living there, it'll only be temporary."

We sat in silence listening to the furniture groan and rustle. "If we didn't have health insurance," Emma said, "I don't know what we'd be doing right now."

I didn't have health insurance, but I said nothing. All she could think about was that baby, and that's how it's supposed to be. She seemed more uncomfortable and worried as the due date approached. I couldn't imagine. Imagining things was always a problem for me. Like imagining my dad out in the van. Was the sex really that great, worth breaking up the family? See what I mean about fake creamer.

···

. . . or, you go through Chandler Park to Conner past City Airport and back to Mt. Olivet. Rinse, repeat, or, more likely, call it a night.

I got home late, Randy and Emma already in bed. In the fridge, an apple/pumpkin combo on a plate. No whipped cream, but beggars can't be losers, right? Randy knew I could never choose, that I'd always want a little piece of everything.

In the yellow kitchen in the house I grew up in, at the table where I spilled my first Cheerios and drank my first beer, I was eating pie made by a stranger, filling up for the long road ahead.

Maybe I didn't want my own place, okay? Maybe I wanted to stay in my old room forever while everything shifted around me.

Maybe I just wanted my brother to say, "Hey, here's our street," and suddenly swerve back onto the familiar comfort of Outer Drive, where if we were careful and lucky enough to turn when it turned, we'd find our way home.

Acknowledgments

"The Spirit Award." *The Cortland Review*.

"Background Noise." *Flyover Country*.

"The Luck of the Fall." *The North American Review*.

"Attack of the Killer Antz, the Rice Method of Recovery, and Other Fables from the Crypt." *The Slab Review*.

"Single Room." *Superstition Review*.

Other Books by Jim Ray Daniels

SHORT FICTION

The Perp Walk

Eight Mile High

Trigger Man: More Tales of the Motor City

Mr. Pleasant

Detroit Tales

ANTHOLOGY

RESPECT: The Poetry of Detroit Music
    co-edited with M.L. Liebler